Praise for Virginia W.

No Motive for Murder

FIVE STARS "VIRGINIA WINTERS'S excellent writing again enhances the adventures of her genealogist detective, Anne McPhail. While visiting relatives in Bermuda, Anne finds she's the suspect this time and moreover her own life is in danger. Can she find the real murderer in time to save herself?"
— Arline Chase, author of Killraven, Ghost Dancer, and the Spirit series, Spirit of Earth, Spirit of Fire, etc..

The Facepainter Murders

"BOOK 2 IN A GREAT SERIES, from Virginia Winters, that will thrill mystery readers and genealogists alike. Masterful writing that puts all the clues before the reader, but hides them so the ending remains a surprise."
— Arline Chase, author of Ghost Dancer, Killraven, and the Spirit series, Spirit of Earth, Spirit of Fire, Spirit of Wind.

"For those of us who loved Murderous Roots, the first volume of this detective series, let me say that the second volume, The Face-painter Murders, is even better. Darn it all but Virginia Winters is a master of planting hints at the end of each chapter so as to make the act of putting down the novel a near impossible act. I just kept reading. And reading. And enjoying the exploits of Doctor McPhail and company right to the suspenseful conclusion."
---R.B. Fleming, historian, biographer.

"FOUR STARS Recently widowed, Canadian doctor Anne McPhail takes leave to trace her genealogy. Arriving in a small Vermont town her ancestors once lived

in, Anne discovers the body of the librarian she came to meet. Since the police suspect the dead woman may have been using her genealogy expertise to blackmail her clients, they ask Anne to help them reconstruct her research, uncovering several dangerous secrets before finally finding the murderer.

"An enjoyable read for genealogists as you experi- ence Anne's elation when she finally finds the record she was searching for."

Jane Nelson, Amazon Reviews

"FIVE STARS FUN BOOK, especially for a genealogist. There are many trails for the police to follow after a blackmailing librarian is murdered. The characters are interesting and the ones you think will wind up being suspects turn out to be just what they appear to be while others don't. I could not put it down."

Mitzy Moo "Eclectic Reader" Amazon Reviews

"FOUR STARS A clever murder mystery with a win- dow into Canadiana, a small town librarian feels compelled to investigate what appears to be a simple murder.... but clearly isn't. Our unlikely heroine finds her- self in the midst of intrigue, danger, and of course some romance. Written with just the right amount of attention to detail and interspersed with wit and humor, this book should be entertaining for both mystery lovers and genealogy enthusiasts alike."

J. Summers (Florida), Amazon Reviews

"FOUR STARS. Whoever said the life of a small-town librarian must be dull? As cadavers pile up, large sums of money change hands, deliberate "accidents" are narrowly averted and romances begin to blossom, the local police are still no wiser. It's time for an amateur genealogist to step in and help solve the mystery."

Nancy Pratt (France), Amazon Reviews

NO MOTIVE FOR MURDER

Dangerous Journeys, vol. 3

VIRGINIA WINTERS

From The River Publishing

From The River Publishing

26 William Booth Crt. Lindsay, Ontario, Canada

K9V 6E1

ISBN: 9780995920835

❀ Created with Vellum

Dedication

FOR MY FAMILY IN BERMUDA...

Chapter One

S udden rain battered Bermuda that morning, pounding the whitewashed roof on its way to the cistern. Rivulets coursed down the windows. Wind bent the old trees that stood in front of the house, survivors of hurricanes of the last fifty years. Beyond the trees, the whitecaps crashed against the grey dock and up onto the white stones stacked along the shore. Anne turned from the window when she saw the car arrived. Usually she took the bus when she went anywhere without her sister, but this was a taxi sort of day.

A sweeping drive led off the street and around an immense ornamental pond to Hamilton's city hall. At the top of the welcoming arms staircase, two-story white pillars guarded the doors. A replica of the ship Discovery decorated the summit of the clock tower, gleaming in the sudden sunshine. Below it the clock with its sea-blue face chimed ten o'clock.

Wide Bermuda cedar stairs, carpeted in deep red, led up from the foyer to an encircling mezzanine. Anne paused to admire the portraits of a young Queen Victoria and Prince Albert, copies of the Winterhalter oils that hung in Windsor Castle that flanked the entrance to the National Art Gallery.

She spent a pleasant but solitary two hours in the permanent collection of paintings, furniture and objets d'arte made by Bermuda artists or inspired by the islands. At noon, she thanked the volunteer at the desk and signed the guest book. There was still time to see an exhibition of art by local children that hung in a room at the other end of the mezzanine. She opened the door.

A scene from a movie. The sound effect, a muffled explosion. One man down, the other searching his pockets. She, screaming, frozen for a moment.

He heard her, jerked his head towards her and away and fled through the exit door. She raced across the endless meters that separated her from the young black man crumpled on the floor.

She pulled off her jacket and knelt by his body; blood was spurting from the hole in his navy tee shirt. The wound punctuated the proud words written on his shirt—Bermuda Born. So young she thought. So young. The soft white cotton of her jacket, pressed against his chest, turned red beneath her hands. His fading heart fluttered and stopped; colour faded from his lips; the pupils in his dark brown eyes dilated. She started chest compressions, but she knew it was too late. The bullet must have gone straight through his heart.

He had no chance. No chance.

"Help," she screamed again. "Help me!"

Blood seeped from beneath the body and congealed on her yellow linen skirt — a thickening, dull-red jelly. A man in a grey uniform, perhaps a security guard, appeared at the top of the staircase, ran towards her along the blue carpet, stopped, his mouth opened to speak, and then he wheeled into the Art Gallery.

Where was he going? Couldn't he see she was in trouble?

A woman appeared in the gallery door, the volunteer from the desk inside, gasped and disappeared.

"Stop. Come back."

Hours passed, or so it seemed. The movements developed an automatic rhythm, useless, but automatic. Sweat dripped into her eyes and her shoulders ached. Her own heart beat a frantic rhythm too, but she couldn't stop; didn't want to let him go. The iron smell of blood, mixed with a faecal stench rose from the body. She gagged and turned aside, afraid she would vomit into the wound, and then started again. At last two paramedics reached her and one took her place on the body. A few people — the volunteer from the gallery, the security guard, three others — stood watching from the safety of the gallery door.

Anne sat back against the wall and pulled in her feet, away from the blood that seemed to creep towards her. The man—the shooter —looked back at her when she shouted at him, wrenched something from his victim's hand and ran to the exit: a strange man— white skin and white hair beneath a ball cap. Something odd about his walk, not a limp, exactly. His gait was uneven, a slight hesitation with his right leg. She thought she'd seen him before. But where and when?

She watched the familiar routine of intravenous fluids and cardiogram and then the final decision that he was gone. A second crew arrived and another paramedic came to her. Anne stood up to speak to him and then sat down and folded her arms into her suddenly cold body.

"I'm a doctor," she introduced herself. "His heart stopped about 11:47."

A uniformed policeman asked her to come with him.

They walked through into the gallery and behind the counter to a small office. Anne sat in an green upholstered chair, opposite a young woman taking notes.

"I'm Deputy-Inspector Spottiswood, of the Serious Crimes Unit," said the woman. "I understand you found the body. May I have your name please?"

"I'm Anne McPhail. I'm a physician. He was alive when I got to him but died moments later."

"Residence?"

The woman kept her head down while she scribbled in a black-covered notebook, the kind workmen used to keep track of their hours. Anne gave her sister's address and added that she was visiting Bermuda from Canada.

"What is your address in Canada?"

Still no eye contact. Was it some kind of investigatory technique, or was the detective just a rude woman? She gave the address of her house in Bridgenorth, in Ontario. She focused on the view of blue sky and white roofs visible through the window behind her questioner. Still the woman kept her dark head bent, her gaze on the stubby yellow pencil in her hand and on the words she was adding. Her writing was almost printing. She added a star to one line, then another. What did she say that was so important, Anne wondered.

"And your business address?"

"I've retired,"

"Say again."

"I said that I've retired."

"Aren't you a little young for retirement?"

The woman raised one eyebrow, and her gaze flickered towards the constable standing behind Anne.

"Perhaps."

What concern was that to the police? Anne could feel the heat rising in her face and knew it would be flaming red in a few seconds. When was this woman going to get past the irrelevant?

The questions that followed were more of the same: exact details of when she arrived; what pictures she looked at; where she was going when she left, and so on.

"Did you recognize the man who ran away?"

Anne turned to look at the woman and found brown eyes staring into hers. They should have been soft, to match her wide mouth and neatly rounded chin, but they were, not hard, but unyielding.

"No, or rather he reminded me of a man I sat beside on the plane yesterday."

"What did he look like?"

"I can describe the man on the plane, but I had only the briefest glimpse of the one who ran out of here this morning. Certainly not enough to swear that it was the same man. He — the man on the plane — was over six feet, average weight for that height, white hair, thick, pale skin. He could have been albino except his eyes were grey, not blue."

"What reminded you?"

"Just his walk, or rather his run. He pushed past me on the gangway from the plane and I watched him walk across the tarmac, and it was the same gait, or so I thought. The man who shot the boy was about the same height and weight, and I think his hair was white, but he was wearing a ball cap, so I'm not sure."

"What was wrong with his gait? Was he crippled in some way? Use a cane?"

"None of that. A little hesitation on the right."

"Not really enough."

"As I said."

Anne waited again for the yellow pencil to catch up with what she'd said. The view out the window hadn't changed, except for a tiny spot of orange on one roof. Anne watched it creep across the white tiles. A ginger cat she thought, hunting.

"Did you know the victim?"

"No."

She saw a brief change of expression on the other woman's face. She didn't believe her, Anne thought, and felt her chest tighten.

"We'll need to search you, Doctor."

"What? Why?"

"We have to ascertain whether or not anyone on the scene has a gun. Please go with the constable."

Anne handed over her purse and her raincoat. She was wearing a simple short-sleeved blue shirt and pale yellow skirt, or at least it had been yellow. Little room to conceal a weapon, she thought, but a woman constable took her into the gallery of children's art, and waited until she stripped to her underwear and dressed again in a set of hospital greens. At least no body cavity search.

"I need to wash."

"We have to check you hands and fingernails, so no washing right now."

"You have no idea whether this young man had infectious disease."

"Take it up with the Inspector."

The Deputy Inspector started again when they joined her.

"Why are you on Bermuda?"

"Before we go on, I need to clean my hands."

"Soon enough."

"Now."

The Inspector, looked again at the standing male constable, who left and returned with a scene of the crime technician. When he finished, he handed Anne wipes and disinfectant for her hands.

"Why are you on Bermuda?"

"Visiting my family."

"So why aren't you visiting them?"

"My sister works mornings, and I wanted to visit the gallery. I'm supposed to meet her for lunch. She's called me several times, I'm sure, but you have my cell phone. She'll come looking for me any moment."

"Is your sister a Bermuda citizen?"

Anne wondered what difference that made, but answered, "Yes."

She gave her sister's name and that of her brother-in-law and the name of his business.

"I would like my belongings back now, and I would like to call my sister." She stood up.

"You expect me to take your word for all of it: the man who ran away; the time of death; how long you spent in the gallery."

The detective was standing now, leaning over the desk that separated them.

"As to the last, I spoke to the volunteer on the desk in there, when I went in and said good-bye when I left. I was the only visitor so perhaps she'll remember me. As to the time of death, the EMS attempted to resuscitate him. I expect they don't usually try that on the long dead. As to the first, yes you only have my word. When you check on me, you'll find my word is good."

"We'll ask you to surrender your passport, which I see you're not carrying."

"Does Bermuda law require that I carry it at all times?"

"No."

"I'll surrender it after I speak to my consulate and a lawyer. I would like my cell phone back, please."

"We've bagged it as evidence."

"Evidence of what? I would like a receipt."

A uniformed police officer spoke to the detective and handed her an evidence bag.

"Do you recognize this, Doctor McPhail?"

Anne could see a gun of some sort, fitted with what she assumed was a silencer, through the dull plastic.

"I know nothing about guns and I certainly don't recognize that one. I'm a physician, Detective. I don't shoot people. My job is to save them."

"It was found outside the exit door. Why would that mysterious man of yours have left his weapon behind?"

"Again, I have no idea...and he's not my man."

"We'll be checking it for fingerprints and DNA."

"You won't find mine."

A constable whispered into Spottiswood's ear.

"Your sister is at the front door. You can go now, Doctor, but don't leave Bermuda. If you try, we will stop you and we will arrest you."

Anne could sense the other two police in the room watching her, waiting for her reply. She caught a raised- eyebrow glance between the two men.

"Stop threatening me, Deputy Inspector. I did nothing except to

7

find this unfortunate young man. My lawyer will be in touch regarding my passport and my phone."

At that Anne turned and stalked past the other two police, under the yellow tape and down the stairs. She could see Liz beyond the front door. A knot of police and others Anne thought were reporters stood between them. A fair-haired woman stepped forward and the man beside her started his camera recording.

"Doctor McPhail, Doctor McPhail. Can you describe what happened for us? Who was shot? Do you know him?" the English voice demanded.

How the hell did they get her name all ready? Did the police give it to them? Maybe the woman in the gallery?

"No comment," Anne said. She could see Liz again, a glimpse of her blonde head through the throng of yelling reporters. Anne turned to a policeman who cleared a path through the crowd for her.

"What happened?" Liz began when Anne reached her. "Are you hurt?"

"No. Get me out of here. I have to talk to you and Dave. I need a lawyer."

Anne forced the words out past a constriction in her throat, and willed herself to breathe.

"What happened?" Liz asked again, when the car doors closed them in. Her pale brows knitted above worried blue eyes.

"I found a man shot up there. He died before I could do more than try to stop the bleeding. A young man, Liz, no older than Martin."

She brushed away tears and leaned forward into her hands.

"Who was he?" Liz took her hand off the key and waited.

"Drive, drive. I don't want to stay here any longer."

"Who was he?" Liz pulled away from the curb and into the airport traffic.

"I don't know. If the police know, they didn't say. And the investigator, a woman called Spottiswood, is threatening me with arrest if

I try to leave the island. And she wants me to surrender my passport!"

"Can she do that?"

"I have no idea. That's why I have to go to the consulate and get a lawyer."

"I think we have to talk to Dave and Martin."

"That too."

"Do you want to go home first? Clean off the blood?" Anne pulled down the sun visor. Her face was smeared with blood; the platinum streak in her hair thick, brown and matted.

"The police didn't take me to a washroom, even after I was searched. They took scrapings from under my fingernails and swabbed my hands and arms for gunshot residue. They gave me wipes for my hands but said nothing about blood on my face. And then they let me walk out, blood all over me. And someone gave the press my name. The pictures in the newspapers will convict me."

"Don't start, Anne. Don't jump ahead. You're not arrested, after all."

"That woman frightened me."

At Dave's office, the assistant stood up and walked around her desk to shake hands with Liz.

"Madeline, is Dave free? We have to speak to him. This is my sister, Anne McPhail."

"His meeting will be over in a few minutes. I'll tell him that you're here. Can I do anything else for you? Tea?"

Her gaze dropped to Anne's still grubby hands and then her streaked face.

"Something stronger?"

"Tea." Anne sank into a metal armchair. The dark green fabric of the back and seat felt rough through the thin cotton of the hospital greens.

"Do you want to clean up? There's a full bath attached to the office," Liz asked again.

"Yes."

But cleaning up had to wait. Dave opened the door behind the assistant's desk. He towered over her five- foot-two sister. His dark blue eyes, brilliant in his tanned face, narrowed when he saw Anne.

"What's going on? Anne, are you hurt?"

"No, no."

"In your office," Liz commanded.

Dave raised his eyebrows but followed along as she ploughed through the door and along the hall to his expansive corner office. High windows on two sides gave views of the harbor and the city, and let in the light needed for his work. Two junior architects stood over a model of an office building. Dave asked them for a few minutes privacy and after a glimpse of Anne's face, they scuttled out the door.

"What the hell?"

"Anne found another body."

Liz collapsed into a black leather visitor's chair near Dave's desk. Anne took another. Dave stood in the window, looking, or so it seemed, across the harbor. He was curly-haired and blue-eyed, tanned and cheerful, middle-height and middle-aged. Took care of himself, Anne saw — a little midriff spread but not much — testimony to the benefits of sailing and Bermuda's hilly landscape.

"Where were you?" he asked when he turned around.

"At the art gallery. When I walked out of the gallery I heard something, like a muffled gunshot. There were two men, one lying on the floor, the other rifling through the fallen man's pockets. When I reached the one on the floor, he was gone. There was nothing I could do for him. He'd been shot, straight through the heart it looked like. I called for help and the paramedics and the police came. A woman called Spottiswood is the investigator and she told me not to try to leave the island and said they would want my passport. Can she do that without charging me with anything?"

"You're a witness. She won't want to let you go."

"They found a weapon outside the exit door. She showed it to me. A gun with a tube attached to the barrel, a silencer, I suppose.

"The gun's not connected to you, so try not to worry," Liz said.

"I need to talk to the consulate."

"Ken Marshall's a good solicitor. I'll call him," said Dave.

"I don't understand why I need one. I've done nothing. They did the test to see if I'd fired a gun."

"Accomplice," Dave said.

"What?"

"They may think you're an accomplice."

Wind, whipping torrential rain against her bedroom window, woke Anne the next morning. Black clouds and rain, she thought. Perfect. The weather was tracking her mood. She caught a glimpse of the angry sea through a moon gate in the stacked stone wall that surrounded the property. She jerked the drapes closed. She wanted off the island; wanted to go home to Canada, to her safe little house.

Liz knocked and carried in a jaunty orange tray laden with a white china teapot and two cups. She sat it down on a glass-topped table in front of the window and handed Anne a cup decorated with roses and took one, daisies, for herself, then opened the drapes. She looked casually elegant in a soft blue dress and jacket in a darker shade.

Anne scowled at the open window. "You're up early," she said.

"I have to go to work."

"You're not coming to the lawyer, then? I hoped you would be able to."

She pushed away her cup and gripped her hands together until the knuckles turned white.

"No, but Dave stayed home. He'll go with you."

"I hope the lawyer believes me."

"Whether he does or doesn't, his job is to give you advice."

"If he doesn't, how can I expect the police to?"

"Come on, Anne. You should wait to worry about whether or not he believes you until after you meet him. The office is in Hamilton, but I'll see you at home afterwards. Try to relax a little. This isn't like you."

"It is though. I had the same reaction in Vermont, the first time."

Anne dressed for her meeting in a dark green skirt, celery-colored cotton sweater and a jacket that matched the skirt. She added a single gold chain, and wore the ruby and diamond engagement ring that Michael had given her, on her right hand. She struggled a little to get it over the knuckle. Her professional self looked back at her from the mirror. A uniform always helped, she thought.

She sat across the breakfast table from Dave, nibbled toast, and picked at a dish of mango slices and strawberries. He was a man who never sugarcoated anything, so Anne was certain of blunt answers to her questions.

"Is he a criminal lawyer?"

"You mean does he do the courtroom work?"

"Yes."

"No. He briefs the barrister if it were to come to that. He's a very good lawyer, Anne. Tough and well- respected."

"I still can't believe I'm in this position. What is wrong with that woman? Why did she leap to the conclusion that I must be involved, without knowing the first thing about me?"

"I don't know anything about her, but the lawyer might. We should get going."

Sunshine replaced the wind and rain by the time they left the house. Anne loved the quirky streets in Bermuda: the circular mirrors mounted at intersections; the stone walls, draped in flowers; the morning glories climbing the telephone poles and creeping out along the wires. The street names intrigued her—Flowercote Lane was a favorite. That morning she didn't see any of them.

The lawyer's office inhabited the penthouse level of a four-story building on Church Street. The architect must have been striving for a Caribbean look, Anne thought, judging by the balconies that punctuated the facade, and the deep-set windows, Small projections from the roof-line, on the other hand, suggested a gesture towards the crenulations of English castles. Perhaps it was a new school, Interpretive Caribbean Architecture, or some such.

They took the elevator to the third floor and walked up to the fourth. The foyer, guarded by a single receptionist, opened into a large room, filled with light and sunshine from the tall windows on three sides. Low partitions separated the space into cubicles. Law books lined the walls between and under the windows. The four partners' offices were along the remaining side, with the two seniors in the corners and the juniors in the center.

The lawyer, Ken Marshall, furnished his space in the old-fashioned way — dark wood furniture and bookshelves, comfortable leather chairs for himself and the client. Pictures of his family occupied a shelf in one corner, visible from his spot behind the desk.

He took the details in the old way too, longhand on a legal-sized yellow pad. Was there a whole industry devoted to creating these pads for lawyers all over the world, Anne wondered, or just Western ones? She liked him: his handshake; his reading glasses, pulled from a desk drawer when she started her story; his deep voice.

"Can they legally take my passport? And should I speak to the consulate?"

"Yes, they can take your passport, but let's wait for an official request. The consulate should know about the trouble. Their office in New York handles Bermuda, but there is an on-island Honorary Consul. I'll call her. If she wants or needs to see you, I'll let you know."

He was taking charge in his lawyerly way, but that meant she would get her money's worth, not that she would be safe.

"I told the detective you would be in touch."

"Clients say and do many things without discussing it with us first. We can ignore that. Don't speak to them again without me there."

"Do I have the right to ask that you be contacted if they arrest me or take me in for questioning?"

"Yes, you do, if you were arrested. If they ask you to come in for questioning, call me before you go. If they take you, but don't give you time to call, say nothing whatsoever but to ask that I be called."

"Won't they think I'm guilty of something if I behave like that."

There was that case of the nurse in Ontario accused of murdering babies. The press and the crown attorney used the fact that she asked for a lawyer immediately as evidence of guilt. And her roommate was a lawyer! Kafka would have understood.

"Answering questions without advice is dangerous, I urge you to call me."

"I will." He handed her his card, wrote a night phone number on the back, and got down to the business of a retainer, which they paid at the desk. Anne's hand shook a little as she signed the credit card slip for the five- figure fee.

"Do I get some of this back it were to turn out that I didn't need much legal help?" she asked.

"Oh, certainly," said clerk.

On the way down in the elevator, Dave told Anne not to expect to see much of the ten thousand again. His son Martin met them at the door when they reached home.

"Dad, the dead guy is Nathan Smith."

"Nathan Smith?"

"You remember, we looked at his paintings last weekend at the fair. The news said the police thought the death was drug-related. He was a good guy. He didn't do drugs."

Anne could hear the outrage in his voice.

"You know they always say that now. Was he a good friend? I don't remember you talking about him."

"No. We knew some of the same people. He lived at home with his mother and worked on one of the big estates as a gardener and he painted."

Martin had dark curly hair and sea-blue eyes like his father and a mouth that was serious most of the time. His smiles were rare, sudden and dazzling. Not that day.

"I should visit his mother. I'm sure she would want to know that he didn't suffer," Anne said.

"I don't think the police would like that," Dave said.

"Why not?"

"Collusion between witnesses."

"For God's sake, Dave. His mother and the woman who held him as he died. You can't be serious."

Anne started pacing the length of the room, pausing to gaze at the Sound for a few seconds, then turning back towards the others.

Liz came in from the kitchen and said, "What's all this uproar about?"

"I want to talk to the boy's mother and Dave thinks the police wouldn't like it."

"You have to be careful, Anne. You're not at home."

"I'm beginning to understand that."

"A bike turned into the driveway," Martin said. "Are we expecting someone?"

"No."

A tiny black woman parked her bike and stood for a moment, looking away from the house towards the Sound, letting the onshore wind blow into her face. She turned and walked up the stairs to the front door. Liz waited for the doorbell to ring and then a few seconds more before she opened it.

"I'm Margaret Smith, Nathan's mother. Could I speak to Doctor McPhail?"

"Yes, of course."

She sat on the sofa, a dark figure in sweater and slacks, a pair of red barrettes in the corn rows that marched across her fine-boned head betraying a taste for color. Perhaps these were her only clothes that weren't vibrant, Anne thought. She sat down beside her and waited silence. Liz brought in tea and only then did Mrs. Smith speak, her voice heavy, weighed with sadness and tears.

"The police said you were with my boy when he died."

"Yes, I was."

"That detective, Spottiswood, she told me not to talk to you. Why did she say that? Does she think you killed Nathan." Her voice trembled and her eyes searched Anne's face.

"I didn't, Mrs. Smith. I'm a doctor from Canada. I came to visit my family. I was only at the gallery to look at the art." Anne leaned forward and touched the woman's large-knuckled hand.

"So was Nathan," she said, and tears overflowed her eyes and coursed down her cheeks. Anne waited.

When Mrs. Smith was calmer, she said to Anne, "Tell me what happened."

"I came out of the art gallery and saw two men on the mezzanine. One of them slumped to the floor and the other ran out through the exit. I saw that Nathan was bleeding badly from the wound in his chest, and I tried to help him. He wasn't conscious and if he suffered it was only for a moment.

A guard came and looked and a woman from the gallery. They must have called the emergency services because the paramedics came and then the police."

"You don't know who did it?"

"No. I only had a brief glimpse of his face."

"Was he a white man?"

The image of the man's face, dead white skin under a navy-blue ball cap with its New York Yankees logo came into focus in her memory.

"Yes. Yes he was."

"Do you have any idea who would want to kill him?"

"No. There's a girl at Tucker's Point."

Anne knew that the ultra-rich from many countries kept homes in the exclusive enclave of Tucker's Point.

"How did he meet her?" Anne asked.

"He works on her family's estate. He wanted to have some connection to land that should have been ours." She lifted her head to look at Dave, as though he would understand.

"What do you mean?" he asked.

"Nathan and I have been searching the land records and the genealogy records for years, trying to find what happened to the land our ancestors owned here."

"Sold?" Dave asked.

"No. No. We couldn't find anything about a sale, and my grandmother told me the land was stolen from us. I'm not very good at this research and Nathan was more interested in his art. After he met Candice, he told me not to worry, that the land would be ours when he married her. He was such a dreamer."

"Was he seeing Candice Wainwright?" Martin said. "Yes."

"He was dreaming. Her father wouldn't let her marry a local."

"How could he stop it?" Liz asked.

"He'd cut her off. Money is very important to Candice. She would never marry anyone without her daddy's approval."

"Nathan told me they were in love," Nathan's mother said.

Anne saw Liz give Martin a little kick and a look that told him to stop talking.

"Maybe Anne could help you with your research," Dave said. "She has a lot of experience."

"I don't know anything about Bermuda genealogy," Anne said.

"You know how to dig."

"That would be wonderful. I want to know," Margaret said, "I want to know if Nathan and I were right. I don't expect to get any land back. Could you help me?"

"Perhaps. I'll let you know," Anne said.

Margaret was satisfied with that. Dave called her a taxi and waited outside with her until it arrived.

"What were you thinking?" Anne asked Dave when he came back in the house. "When I start to look at someone else's genealogy, I always get into some kind of trouble."

"If the land should belong to her, it would be helpful to know that."

"Helpful to whom?"

"To you. As a motive for murder that doesn't involve you."

Chapter Two

Earlier that same day, Adrienne Spottiswood left city hall, skirted the fountain and its turbulent pool, crossed the street and took the stairs down to the next street. Halfway down, three plastic chairs and a solitary table sat outside a restaurant door, pretending they were on a sun-drenched terrace. Paula sat in one of the chairs, separated from the street by a potted hedge of evergreens. The better to be seen, Adrienne thought, noting the other woman's tied-back long blond hair, the faded shirt that outlined her breasts and proclaimed her an admirer of "Tall Ships, Bermuda" and the makeup that accentuated long black eyelashes and painted her mouth vermillion.

"So is it your case?" The English voice, usually abrasive and loud, rumbled the question, an apparent attempt to be discreet.

"Yes, so far."

"What have you done now to piss them off?"

"I interviewed the only witness, and apparently I was too aggressive."

"Did she do it?"

"I think so, but no one else does."

"What do you know about her?"

"Nothing much. She's the sister-in-law of that

architect, Heath. She's supposed to be visiting. She's not talking to me without her solicitor."

"Why would she if you practically accused her of murder?" Paula said with a glance at the approaching server.

"I think the department's stonewalling me already."

"Why? Don't they want the case cleared?"

"They want me cleared out, but they're afraid of backlash."

"As they should be. My paper would make quite a big deal of that. I'll look for information about her."

"You let me know what you find."

"Make that a request, not an order."

"Please."

Adrienne's phone vibrated; she took the call and had to go.

"I'll call you," Paula promised.

An hour later she was knocking on Mrs Smith's door. "Mrs Smith? I'm Paula Benson of the Bermuda Reporter. Could I talk to you for a few minutes?"

"No." Her voice dragged, and Paula thought she might be sedated.

"Just a word. Do you believe the McPhail woman had anything to do with your son's death?"

"No. She tried to help him. I've talked to her, and she told me what happened." Margaret started to swing the door shut.

"Wait. Then you think the police are on the wrong track?"

"They won't even listen. My boy was killed because of the land. I'm sure of it."

"What land?"

"Good-bye." The door slammed shut.

Paula walked away, turning off the powerful but tiny recorder she concealed in her pocket. A story was forming. All it needed was a little information on Doctor McPhail.

Although the Bermuda Reporter was very small, an upstart in the cozy world of Bermuda journalism, where the Royal Gazette, the opposition, had existed for more than a hundred and eighty years, she hoped to make a mark big enough to be seen by another, bigger paper. If not the UK papers of her dreams, at least an American paper, or a Canadian one. A story about a Canadian doctor, a woman, a murder suspect, might be enough. And she had the inside edge, what with Adrienne's discontent with how she was being treated by the force. Paula slipped into the chair in her grey-walled cubicle, three feet away from the corner office with the window and the desk with three phone lines and two computer screens that she coveted. Not perhaps that office but one like it, somewhere, anywhere else. The screen on her Mac waited for her input; its icons lined up in glowing rows. She hit Dogpile, to search several engines at once and input Anne McPhail's name. Four pages into the search, she found a reference to a newspaper in Vermont and the second of the two murders Anne was involved with there.

Not too bad, she thought. She would give some of it to Adrienne. Not the part in which the doctor, a hero, solved the mystery and recovered a letter written by Paul Revere, but the facts that she visited the town twice and found bodies both times. She would save the hero aspect for her story.

She texted Adrienne to call her and sat back and waited.

"What are you doing in here," her boss bellowed across the room at her. "I thought you were on that murder at the art gallery?"

"I am. I—"

"Save it. Let me read it," He disappeared into his office. The door slammed behind him.

Someday, someday, she would slam that door in his thirty-two-year-old, overbearing, narcissistic, weak-chinned face, on her way out and onto a flight to...Florida. Yes, Florida would be good. She'd like to live there, working on one of the dailies. Her phone rang its happy drumbeat, breaking into her daydream.

"What?" Adrienne said.

Rude, Paula thought.

"Deputy-Inspector Spottiswood, I have some information for you."

"Yes?"

Still rude. Couldn't she take a hint?

"The McPhail woman was involved in two murders in Vermont. Both times she found the body. Worth a question or two."

"What details have you found?"

"That's about it," she lied.

"Thanks, Paula. I owe you lunch."

"You owe me a scoop."

Adrienne hung up and a few minutes later was knocking on Liz's front door.

Anne ran her hands over the cold, blue-streaked, white marble of the dining table in the garden, and watched the kiskadees flit in and out of Liz's prized snowberry bushes. From a neighboring rooftop a mourning dove called.

Genealogy in the context of a murder investigation was dangerous. It only brought her trouble in the past. Who knew what could happen here if she started to dig? How many people, most of all the police would she annoy. The screen door slammed behind Liz. Vivid red blotches marred her fair skin and the chair she pulled out protested with an angry screech.

"What's happened?"

"Spottiswood is here to see you."

"Did she say she has a warrant?"

"No."

"Call the solicitor."

Anne stood up, straightened her shoulders, smoothed her skirt, tugged at her jacket and strode into the living room. The detective, accompanied by a young man she didn't introduce, told her she a few questions.

"I would be happy to talk to you with my solicitor present but not otherwise."

"What have you got to hide, Doctor?"

"Nothing, but I'm not a citizen of Bermuda, and I understand that the rights of your constitution don't extend to visitors. So I need to see to my protection."

"Has your sister called him?"

"Yes."

Liz walked in and told Anne that the lawyer would arrive in a few minutes.

"Quick service," commented the detective. "I understand finding dead bodies is a hobby of yours."

One of her sister's little kicks reminded Anne of her promise to say nothing.

The doorbell rang.

The lawyer came in, recognized the detective and said, "Good afternoon, Deputy-Inspector. What can we do for you?"

"Mr Marshall. Your client has a habit of finding dead bodies. This is the third. Perhaps she could explain that to us."

Anne hadn't mentioned the two previous murder investigations in Vermont that each began with her finding a body and ended with her helping in the hunt for the killer. The lawyer told Spottiswood he needed a minute.

"What is she talking about? Something you forgot to tell me?" he said when they were in the kitchen.

"I happened to stumble across two bodies, two separate times in Vermont. I wasn't a suspect, but I was involved with the investigations. If she called the police there, she would have known that. She's only Googled and found a newspaper article or something that mentioned me. The police there will speak for me."

"Then tell her all about them."

Anne sat down across from the detective. "What would you like to know?" she asked.

"Tell me about the other bodies."

Anne told her about the cases as they developed and her involvement in them.

She found the body of a murdered librarian, a genealogical researcher in the library of the small Vermont town of Culver's Mills. Her research helped solve the case but brought her close to losing her own life.

Eighteen months later she found the body of a naked man lying in a ditch that bordered her friend's property in the same Vermont town. Again her skill at genealogical research helped reveal not only the killer but a treasure trove of historical arte-facts. It also brought her into the sights of a seasoned killer. She gave the names of the Chief of Police and the detectives she worked with.

"You worked for the police?"

"With them, yes. I didn't get paid if that's what you were asking."

"Because you're an expert in genealogy?"

"Knowledgeable, not an expert."

"Whatever."

She'd been looking around the spacious, comfortable room while Anne was talking. Several pieces of Bermudian art hung on the walls. "I see your family enjoys art as well as you?"

"Yes."

"The young man who died was an artist. You hadn't met him?"

"No."

"Or his family?"

"His mother came here this morning."

"Yes, even though I told her no contact."

"Perhaps you did, but she wanted to talk to the person who'd been with her son when he died. I think she wanted to make her mind up about me. I was able to answer her questions and assure her that he hadn't suffered. Would you have turned her away at the door?"

The young woman, and Anne realized that she was in fact quite young to be lead detective on a murder case, flushed and didn't answer.

"Is that all?" the solicitor asked.

"Yes, for now."

Anne turned to the lawyer when the door closed behind the police.

"Why is she focused on me? I don't think she even listened when I told her about the man who ran from the body?"

"You were there, Anne, and only you. They have to consider you," the lawyer said.

"I never met that young man. I didn't know his name until Martin told me. All I tried to do was save his life."

"They won't be able to connect you, and that will be the end of it. Remember to say nothing without me present."

"All right. I have a flight home the day after tomorrow. What shall I do about that?"

"Can you stay?"

"Yes, but I don't want to."

"Change your ticket to a week from now, and we'll see how things are going."

"Fine."

The solicitor left; Dave and Martin went to work; Anne and Liz sat in the kitchen, at a pine table in the bow window. The kitchen extended the width of the house and overlooked the garden. Liz had painted the cabinets a willow green and the walls cream. One of her collection of crystal perfume bottles, which sat on glass shelves in front of a window, broke the sunshine and stained the walls with a rainbow of colors.

"What are you going to do about Mrs Smith?" Liz asked after a few moments of silence.

"I don't know. I need to do something while I wait for them to arrest me. Genealogy would be time- consuming and get me out of your hair every day."

"They're not going to arrest you."

"I think she might try. I saw that man before, the one who shot the boy," Anne said.

"You did? Where?"

"On the plane. You remember that man who pushed past me on the stairs from the plane?"

"Yes."

"I think it was him. Those same nasty, cold, little shark's eyes and that white hair."

"Are you sure?"

"No."

The phone in Anne's pocket vibrated its alert. When she answered, it was to hear Thomas's voice.

"Hi, dear heart. How are you?"

"Thomas." Anne fought back her sudden tears.

"What's the matter?"

"I've found another body and the police think I'm involved in the murder." She pushed the words out past the obstruction forming in her throat, the one that took her words and her breath when she was frightened or angry or sad.

"Where are you?"

"At my sister's."

"What's the address? I'll be there as soon as I can."

"Where are you? New York?"

"No. The Bermuda Airport."

Anne told him the address and then looked over at Liz.

"Thomas?" Liz said.

"A man I've seen since that first visit to Vermont. He's a businessman."

"You didn't say anything?"

"I know how much you liked Michael. I was worried you'd think it was too soon."

"For heaven's sake, Anne. Five years! I was more worried that you hadn't moved on. What's he like?"

"His name is Thomas Beauchamp. Fifty, five-ten, dark hair, dark eyes, big nose. He works between New York and Toronto and his mother lives in Vermont. He has three grown children, but his wife died many years ago."

"What else? Do you love him?"

"I don't know yet."

Anne watched at the window that overlooked the drive the street beyond and the water of Harrington Sound beyond that. A taxi crunched to a stop on the gravel of the driveway. She flew out the front door, down the steps and into Thomas's arms.

"Tell me what happened."

They sat on the low stone wall that separated the terrace from the lawn while Anne told him about the discovery, the interviews, her fear.

"What about the solicitor? I could have someone from the New York office here tomorrow."

"Dave got him for me and said that he has the reputation of being an excellent solicitor. I thought he was sensible and tough. The detective was...deferential."

She stood up and brushed herself off. "My sister will be wondering."

After the first few moments, Liz and Thomas were chatting like old friends.

"What are you doing here, Thomas?" Liz asked.

"I came in for a business meeting. It was arranged at the last minute," he said, turning to Anne, "and so I thought I would surprise you. I wanted to ask you if you would come to the dinner with me at the Wainwright estate."

"Wainwright! That's the name of the girl the dead boy was supposed to be seeing," Liz said.

"Might be interesting," Anne said.

"Shall I pick you up at seven?" Thomas asked. "Oh, black tie," he added. His taxi returned, and he was gone.

"Black tie. What am I going to wear?"

"Let's check the closet."

Shoes were the only problem, and they solved that with a quick shopping trip to Hamilton. Anne and Liz were the same height, only five two, and the same weight. As teens, they were mistaken for twins, and often wore each other's clothes and still could.

At seven Anne clasped one of her sister's gold chains around her neck and adjusted the collar of her white silk shirt. Liz's ankle-length, blue cocktail suit fit her perfectly.

"You look great," Liz said.

"Thanks to your clothes. Why do men think they can surprise us with sudden invitations to formal affairs?" "Because we keep meeting expectations and saying yes. You'll have gorgeous food and wine."

"Thomas didn't say how large an event this is. I hope big, so I can blend in."

The sun, setting, stained the house on the hill above them vermillion and lavender. They turned off the seaside road into a long gravel driveway overhung with trees. Hostas in shades from golden to deep blue filled the spaces between the trees. They stopped in a circular drive at the foot of an expansive staircase. Anne took Thomas's arm and they climbed up to the accompaniment of music that drifted down through the open doors at the top.

Two men stood at the entrance, checking invitations. Anne noticed that above them, a security camera blinked. Someone, somewhere in the house knew they were there. Thomas turned to shake hands with a man he introduced as Chuck Wainwright, their host. Wainwright, more than six feet tall, very thick fair hair, long prominent ears and a stubborn set to his lower jaw was attractive, Anne thought, but he looked remorseless. She could hear her sister's voice in her head, telling her not to make snap judgments.

He welcomed Anne and started to discuss the coming business meeting with Thomas. Their voices, aimed a foot above Anne's head, were lost in the growing roar of the crowd. After a few minutes, he clasped Thomas by the shoulder and moved away.

They stood on the edge of the sea of guests that spilled from the reception room through a row of open French doors onto a terrace and lawns that overlooked the sea. A passing waiter gave them each a glass of champagne and tacked on through the melee.

First one, then another came up to speak to Thomas, acknowledge his introduction to her and move into what Anne called business-speak. A painting above the fireplace of a lovely child, age perhaps ten, freckled and tanned, standing on a sailboat, took her attention. When she turned back, the crowd had swallowed Thomas. She glimpsed him for a moment before he again disappeared into a throng. She'd let him find her, she thought, and moved to the side where she could watch the crowd.

Tall women, mostly blond, wearing gorgeous gowns, waiters in bright green jackets, all punctuated by the black of the tuxedos, swirled in the light from a single crystal chandelier, more massive than Anne had ever seen in a private home. The evening grew darker; torches lit the terrace.

His stuttering gait drew Anne's attention to a man moving from point to point around the room, keeping to the periphery of the crowd. He stopped to speak to the butler who had greeted them at the door and resumed his slow circle of the room. Two thoughts collided. He was the man from the plane; he was checking the security. And then another, more frightening one. He'd seen her and was moving slowly towards her. She edged away, took her new cell phone from her purse, and snapped a picture of the crowd and him.

Thomas appeared at her side.

"We're going in to dinner," he said. "I'm sorry that I left you for so long."

"So am I," she said. "He's here."

They moved with the crowd to the dining room, another vast area filled with tables for six.

"Who?"

"The man from the gallery. He saw me too."

"You said you only saw the man at the gallery for a moment."

"He recognized me. I could see it in his eyes." "Likely he recognized you as the annoying woman from the plane. Didn't you say you'd laughed at him when he almost fell?"

"Yes. I was in 8-a, and he was in 8-b. When he stood up while we were still landing and the seat belt sign was on, he lurched into his seat and almost into me. He was unpleasant even before that, and then he almost knocked me off the stairs and glared at me as though it were my fault."

"That's what I mean. He knows you as an annoying seat-mate, not a murder witness."

"Thomas, he looked back at me from the exit door at the gallery. He knows I saw him." Her voice started to rise.

"Don't get so upset. Do you want to leave?" Thomas steered them away from the tables and out of the mainstream of the crowd.

"Yes, but aren't you trying to have a business meeting in the midst of all this?"

"I've already talked to the people I came to see."

"If our places are empty, he'll be able to find out who we are."

"Either way he can. Do you see him anymore?"

"No, but I can't see much in this crowd. I'd like to tell the police that I saw him here, but I don't think they'll believe me."

"Let's go find out."

Thomas edged them through to the dining room, found his host, made their apologies and led Anne out a side door and around to the front. They waited a few minutes for a taxi. Anne felt someone watching them from the shadows; saw someone slip back inside.

"I think he was watching us."

"Paranoia?" Thomas said. He took her hand, but she shook him off and turned away.

"No. I saw someone in the shadows."

Spottiswood came to see them at her office, rather than leave them to the duty officer. They'd been with her for half an hour when Anne decided she'd had enough of the fruitless talk and the hard wooden chair that was biting into the back of her thighs. She stood up and waved her phone at the other woman.

"Detective, I took a picture of the man at the party. Do you want to see it or not?"

"What are you trying to do? Distract me from you?"

"I've told you the truth. You'll find nothing that implicates me, and frankly, I think you're taking the lazy way out of this. Blame the person who found the body, especially since she's not Bermudian. That's your approach."

"We'll find your DNA on the body."

"I hope so since I tried to save his life. It takes more than DNA as I'm sure the Director of Public Prosecutions has told you. I'd like to talk to your supervisor, please."

"Why?"

"Because I have information that you are ignoring, because I think that I and by extension my family and Thomas are in danger from this man."

"You have no proof of that."

"I'm a witness here. I'm not the one who is supposed to be looking for evidence. Do you want this picture or not?"

"Send it to me." She gave her business card to Anne.

"Fine." Anne sent the picture from her phone, turned on her heel and stalked out the door. "

That went well," Thomas said.

"Arrogant puppy. I hope that's the last I have to see of her."

But Spottiswood was back at her sister's door the next morning.

"What is it now?" Anne said.

"May I come in?"

"No. What do you want?"

"I want you to look at a picture."

Anne laughed and after a moment the detective laughed with her. Her stern face transformed into that of a happy young woman.

"Come in," Anne said.

"We identified one of the people in the picture you sent as a man suspected of terrorist activities in the U.K. We arrested him last night and put him on a plane this morning."

She handed Anne a page of photos.

"None of these is the man I saw," Anne said, "but I think this one was a waiter, one of the ones carrying around a tray of champagne."

"That's the one we deported."

Adrienne as she asked Anne to call her, passed another photo, an enlargement of the one from her phone.

"This one." Anne indicated the man from the plane.

"We haven't been able to identify him. Perhaps he's one of those obnoxious people, and his face is similar to the man you say ran from the scene."

"I thought he was checking the security."

"You don't know that."

"No."

"Did you check on the man in the seat next to me on the plane?"

"He left the next morning on a flight to New York."

"That can't have been the same man."

"Same passport."

"So is she your new best friend?" Liz asked when they were alone again.

"I think she's been told to change her approach, but she still suspects me."

"I think so too. I bet she'll be back."

Chapter Three

Anne closed her computer, turned off her phone, leaned back in her chair and said to her sister, "I wonder if airlines ever experience lower than normal call volumes. Do you suppose the message would be "Due to lower than normal call volumes, we've all gone for coffee. Please return in one half-hour in order to experience our normal call delay"."

Liz laughed and said, "Did you get the flight changed after all that?"

"Yes, finally."

"What are you doing today?"

"I'm starting the research for Mrs Smith. You?"

"Work. Do you want a drive?"

"No, thanks. I'll take the bus."

A bright pink bus, jaunty with a horizontal blue stripe and darker pink waves painted below that, rounded the corner and stopped for her. She said good morning to the driver and the other passengers — an old man with a gap-toothed smile, a woman in a two-piece suit and formidable brown oxfords, and two hooded teenagers. A chorus of good mornings answered. Anne settled back to enjoy the trip through the winding streets, past high stone walls laden with flowers and down hills and around blind corners. A tiny blue car, parked a few meters away, started its engine and moved in behind the bus.

The main bus terminal, a one-story building with high-domed open slots for the vehicles, sat next to the city hall and across from a park called Victoria. Anne knew it was constructed in Scotland in 1899 and recently sent back there for repairs. She wondered why. Surely it would have been cheaper to bring workmen over from Scotland to fix it. She walked on to a slightly out-of-place modern glass and steel building called Victoria Hall, at 11 Victoria Street. The old Queen certainly left her mark on the island.

The Land Registry Office occupied the third floor. Anne hadn't found anything on-line to help her with the quest she was undertaking for Margaret Smith. She knew that, until recently, the land registry hadn't been centralized and that the process, although underway, was unlikely to help her.

"Good morning," she said to the woman behind the desk. "My name is Anne McPhail. I called yesterday about looking at some of your early land records."

"Yes, of course. We have the record of the original survey, the division into tribes, and then into strips. Which landowner are you researching?"

"All I have is the name Smith and the parish."

"That's a start, although you will find that Smith is a very common name."

And common was what she found. She knew that family legend was often mistaken so thorough research would demand that she look at all people named Smith in the original documents and follow the genealogy of each to determine if Margaret were indeed the rightful heir of any land.

She began with the earliest records, of the initial division of the land into eight "tribes" or parishes, each bearing the name of one of the principal investors in the Bermuda Company. The parishes were further divided into twenty-five-acre pieces and subdivided through the ensuing years.

Starting at the beginning was a mistake. She needed to follow Margaret's genealogy back to her family's arrival on Bermuda. To do that, she needed to talk to Margaret again.

Back at the reception desk, she asked, "Do you have any genealogical records at all? Census, church records, wills…?"

"No. Those are held at the Archive on Parliament Street. Could I call them for you to get any particular record ready?"

"No, thanks. I have to speak to some of the living relatives first, to get an idea of where to start."

Another pink bus dropped her at the bottom of a hill near Devil's Hole, a geological formation resulting from the collapse of a giant sinkhole, now an aquarium. It became Bermuda's first tourist attraction, in 1830.

Margaret's house, a pale blue bungalow, sat at the top of the hill, separated from the road by a short stretch of lawn where a solitary yellow hibiscus bloomed. The address was 37-A, which meant Margaret lived in an apartment carved out of the one-car garage. Anne knew that many homes were, in fact, two-in-one, with the apartment helping to sustain the mortgage.

The door opened before she knocked. Margaret, dressed for company in a black skirt and pale grey blouse, welcomed her.

"Thank you for coming, Doctor McPhail. Please come in."

The door opened straight into the living room. The window that replaced the former garage door, with its view over the treetops to the sea, gave light and air to the cramped space. A taupe sofa against one wall, two dark brown armchairs, a television on a stand in one corner and a pine table large enough for two left only a narrow passage to an arch that opened the kitchen to the front room. A door beside it led, Anne, presumed, to the bedroom and bathroom. Nathan lived here with his mother, so he must have taken the couch.

Paintings, mostly unframed, were stacked against the walls;

some, framed, hung on every available wall space. Nathan's work, she thought, vibrant and joyous.

"I'm sorry to intrude, Margaret."

"No, you're not intruding. You said on the phone that you needed my help in the search. I have all the information we gathered ready for you."

"I need to search your genealogy so that I know whose land we're looking for."

Margaret handed her a shoe box full of yellowed newspaper clippings, everything from death notices to birth announcements to reports of weddings. Deeper in the box she found copies of old wills and mortgages. Her job would be to correlate the two.

"It's your husband's family that I have to research, is it?"

"No, mine."

"So the surname isn't Smith?" Damn, she thought. Starting at the wrong end, with the wrong name. Maybe the lady needed someone else to help her.

"No, Roberts."

"What can you tell me about your family?"

"Let me get some tea."

When Anne left her notebook was filled with Margaret's family history back to the turn of the twentieth century. Margaret knew nothing before that but was certain from the family legend that the land they lost was the very plot on which the Wainwright mansion stood. Anne promised to try to find the truth for her.

Adrienne walked in to the cafe and looked for Paula. She found her at one of the tables perched at the edge of an unprotected terrace. She sat, ordered a lemonade and waved the menu in front of her face. Hotter and more humid than usual for September, the weather was getting stranger. And why was Paula looking so cool, smug and cool?

"What have you found out?" she asked.

"Manners, Adrienne. Not even a hello?"

"I'm in a hurry. What have you go to tell me?"

"I followed the McPhail woman this morning. By the way, I was the only one. Where were your people?"

"Doing their jobs. She's not getting off the island. I can pick her up whenever I want to."

"She went to the Land Registry Office and then to Mrs Smith's. Why would she need to go to the Land Registry?"

"Mrs Smith's obsession. She thinks her family owns the land Wainwright bought."

"And do they?"

"Of course not, Paula. A title search was done."

"Well, you should know," Paula said.

"How long was she at Mrs Smith's?"

"She was still there when I left ten minutes ago."

She was talking to Adrienne's back. Paula started making notes, in the precise script she'd been taught at her school in England. A story was taking shape.

On her way to Liz's home, Adrienne called the office, talked to her boss and received instructions.

Anne walked up the drive towards her sister's house. She felt tired, weighed down. Perhaps it was the weather. The walk from the bus stop left her hair wet against her forehead, sticky with the humidity and sweat. In the past, she'd felt uplifted by the sight of the old, pink, two-story house with its welcoming arms staircase to the front door, but even that didn't help her mood, nor did the sight of Adrienne's dark figure, seated on a bench on the front terrace.

"Again, Adrienne? What is it this time?"

Anne walked past her, up the stairs and into the Georgian hallway. A staircase of Bermuda cedar rose in a gentle curve to the left to a gallery on the second floor. The floor of the foyer was cedar too, covered with a worn but beautiful oriental rug.

"You might as well come in," she said. She deposited her keys on the hall table, missing the crystal base of a ruby-shaded lamp, but kept her briefcase with her. Adrienne followed her down the hall to the kitchen.

Liz looked up from her computer's screen and its image of a recipe she wanted to try.

"What's going on?" she asked.

"I found her in the front garden."

"I have been instructed to tell you formally that you are requested to remain on Bermuda for the present," Adrienne began.

"And if I want to go home?"

"We will be forced to arrest you."

Liz, who was standing behind Anne, picked up the phone and called the solicitor. The other two waited in silence for the conversation to finish.

"Anne, Mr Marshall instructs you to say nothing more to Deputy-Inspector Spottiswood. And he means nothing."

Anne said, "Good day, Adrienne," and left the room. "I need to know your intentions."

"Talk to the lawyer." The door to the bedroom slammed.

"Has she gone?" Anne called, then walked down the stairs at the answer.

"Yes. What do you think brought about yet another change in attitude?"

"I suppose they noticed that I was poking around, visiting the land records office, talking to Mrs Smith. Maybe they're watching her house, or maybe they're following me. I should leave. I can stay with Thomas at his hotel. He wants me to, anyway."

"I thought his business was finished."

"No, there's another meeting at Wainwright's tomorrow, a luncheon this time."

"Are you going?"

"I don't think so. We're having lunch today though. I'll call and suggest I come stay with him. That'll keep the cops from your door."

"It doesn't matter."

"You know it does. This is a small place, and you have Dave's business to think about."

Liz was far from convinced, but when Thomas arrived, Anne was packed.

"I'll call later," she promised.

Thomas's villa nestled in the beautiful gardens of an old hotel. The terrace, furnished with black wrought- iron table and chairs opened onto a sort-of lawn, tufts of grass in the sand, and then the soft-pink beach.

"Spouses have invited to that lunch after all," Thomas said.

Anne shook out a skirt and hung it in the closet. She liked to settle in, even if only for a day or two.

"Do you want me to come?"

"Yes. After lunch, there's a working group and some sort of spousal program. What about it?"

"Spousal program sounds dreary, but I would like to see the estate in the daytime."

"Good. In the meantime, this is a hotel room, this is a bed, and I'm all alone on it."

"We can't have that."

Later, they called for room service and ate lunch on the terrace.

"I have a meeting this afternoon at one of the banks," Thomas said.

"Then I'll go shopping."

"Not genealogy."

"Not today."

A hotel car took them into Hamilton and left them at a cream-painted building, formerly the home of the most prestigious department store on Bermuda, occupied by the largest bank, the Bank of Bermuda.

"Shall I ask the car to return for you?" Thomas asked.

"No, thanks. I'll take the bus."

Under the arches of the portico that fronted the building, Anne paused to decide which direction her ramble should take her. Some of the shops she remembered from previous visits were gone now. Bermuda was hard hit by the economic downturn, and many businesses went under. She wandered along the street, looking in shop windows, and stopped to admire the offerings in a jewelry store. She stepped through the doorway into the old-fashioned store — polished wooden floors and dark, glass-topped locked cabinets, the jewels within set in blue-velvet rows. The clerks were male, dressed in the dark formal length shorts, white shirts and quiet ties that were the uniform of the Bermuda businessman. She saw a familiar face gazing into a case of rings.

"Adam?" He was her friend, Adam Davidson, the detective she worked with in Vermont.

"Hi, Anne. I wondered if we would run into you here. You're in time." He gave her a quick hug.

She looked up into the dark eyes set in a now-tanned face that missed being handsome, thanks to a nose broken on several occasions. In the formal Bermudian atmosphere of the store, he looked big and American and uncomfortable in his dark jeans, green golf-shirt and brown deck shoes.

"In time for what?"

"To help me choose a ring."

Anne knew that he'd come to Bermuda with his girlfriend, Erin Maxwell. Now she knew his reason.

"You're choosing the ring without her?"

"I thought I would. I know she loves estate jewelry and there are cases of it here. But I'm not sure how to narrow it down."

"I'd start with how much you have to spend."

"We've done that."

"Before you choose," she said, "consider if there's one that you would be happy to see on her finger every day."

"Still too hard," he said, looking at a tray with fifty rings set in rows of tens.

"Do you want a diamond or a colored stone?"

"She likes emeralds."

There were three emeralds on the tray, one set off by tiny diamonds, one a single perfect emerald set in platinum and one that Anne called a cocktail ring, ornate with a square-cut emerald surrounded by pave diamonds.

"That one," Adam said, pointing to the single emerald.

"May I see it?" Anne said.

She reached into her purse for the loupe she always carried. She used it for everything from looking at jewels to inspecting antique photographs to deciphering printing on old documents. The lovely emerald, nestled in an exquisite setting of platinum filigree, contained only one tiny inclusion: a measure of the stone's quality.

"It's a natural emerald," the clerk said.

"Beautiful," Anne said. She handed it back to Adam. "I'm sure she would love it."

"If she doesn't or says no, can I return it?" he asked the clerk.

"Of course."

They walked along the sidewalk to a bench that overlooked the harbor. Sailboats, motorboats, one taking tourists on para-sailing adventures, a small ferry crossing to Hamilton from the far reaches of the island, a rare fishing boat or two in sea-dimmed colors of red or blue, distracted Anne for a few minutes. She didn't want to interrupt Adams's perfect day with her problems, but he must have seen something in her face.

"What's the matter?"

"The police here think I might be a murderer."

"Tell me."

Anne told him about the murder she interrupted, and the detective who suspected her. She watched Adam's face for reassurance but no. All she saw was deep concern. Adam was an experienced detective, twelve years on the police force of the small Vermont town of Culver's Mills and a part-time law student.

"Do you want to go see her with me?"

"Do you think that would help?"

"Maybe."

A taxi dropped them in front of the building across from police headquarters where Adrienne had her office.

"She's not in the main building?"

"None of the senior staff are. The Service moved from a more remote location to here, I understand from my brother-in-law."

"Odd."

Adam showed his badge and asked to speak to Adrienne.

"What can I do for you, Lieutenant Davidson?" she asked. She ignored Anne who stood beside and a little behind Adam.

"Just a courtesy call, Deputy Inspector. You know my friend Anne McPhail?"

"Yes."

"Could we have a word with you?"

"Yes. Come with me. What are you doing on Bermuda, Lieutenant?" she asked. She walked them into her office and stood, waiting for the answer. The space was large enough for a small desk, two visitors' chairs in mismatched wood and one behind the desk in faux leather.

It was none of her business, but Adam told her he was there on vacation and met Anne by accident.

"You wanted to know about Anne's history in Vermont?"

"Three bodies in as many years."

"We had a killer loose, twice. Anne helped us bring each of them in."

"However, she is the only person we can place at the scene of this one." Adrienne stood back against her desk.

"Only because you won't believe me. And the only reason you won't believe me, as far as I can see, is my history in Vermont," Anne said. She stood too. Her hands curled into fists at her side.

"Not the only reason. There's a gun at the scene. You've scrapped acquaintance with the dead boy's mother; you're poking into land records; you've been seen at Tucker's Point with no explanation for being there."

"Margaret Smith came to me. I'm looking into land records at her request. As to Tucker's point, if you mean that I was at a dinner there with Thomas Beauchamp, yes I was. What's that to you?"

"You told me you were visiting your family. Suddenly you're a genealogical investigator and attending international meetings with a mysterious American businessman. You lied to me. That's what it is to me."

Anne stood face to face with Adrienne, too close in the small office.

"Let's go, Anne." Adam took her arm.

She shook him off, turned and stalked out across a squad room crowded with desks and police and on out.

"How am I going to get out of this?" Her voice shook.

"Keep under her radar. No poking around."

"I think they're watching me."

"Probably."

Adam insisted on the taxi taking her back to her hotel,"

"Goodbye," Anne said. "Good luck with the big question."

Adam thought the visit to the police was a mistake and he regretted suggesting it. On the other hand, he had the ring in his pocket and soon he would meet Erin for lunch. He was undecided when he would ask her. Night was more romantic, but the sooner he saw the ring out of his pocket and onto her finger, the happier he would be. He was also late for lunch.

Erin was looking out over the sea, her dark head turned away from him. His heart skipped a beat when she turned and smiled at him. He kissed her and started to apologize for making her wait.

"I met Anne. She's in trouble again. Another body."

"No. Where? And who? How is she?"

"In the art gallery in the city hall. He was a young local artist. And she's not very good. The local police are suspicious of her."

"Poor Anne. What do you think?"

"I think I understand why they're looking at her. You and I know she didn't do anything, but for all they know, she could be an accomplice or the killer who dumped her gun and then pretended to be helping her victim. All the emphasis she's placing on a mysterious, dangerous man, could be so much diversion."

"What man?"

"She thinks she recognized the killer. Some guy from her flight down here."

"But if you think that way," she protested, "so will they. How can we help her?"

"We can't."

He watched tears fill her dark eyes. He pushed the ring box deeper into his pocket. The server arrived to tell them his name was Anthony and recite the day's specials.

Anne opened the door to the villa to find only the silent anonymity of a cleaned hotel room. His meeting must have gone late, she thought. She stepped out onto the terrace, taking with her a magazine from the selection in the room. History of Bermuda to the Present Day, the cover read. The words accompanied a photo of the very beach in front of her. She flipped the pages, not focusing on any of the text until she came to an article about the expropriation of land to make way for the Tucker's Town development. The article was written, as histories often were, from the point of view by the victors. All of the people who lost their homes and land were happily settled elsewhere on the island, it claimed. Anne jotted down some of the names. She would eventually have to find other sources of information, to confirm the happy ending the magazine offered. She doubted, from what Mrs Smith told her, that everyone was satisfied with the government's solution.

When she closed the magazine, she saw a Bermuda phone number penciled in Thomas's neat script, with the name Quin beside it. Quin, she thought. Who was Quin? She closed her eyes and let the last of the afternoon sun play on her face. She didn't hear Thomas come in and startled when he spoke.

"I'm sorry. I didn't mean to interrupt your nap."

"Not napping; enjoying the sun."

She sat up to be kissed and then settled back into her chair. Thomas brought out two glasses and bottle of white wine.

"How was your day?" He handed her a glass of wine.

"I met Adam Davidson in a jewelry store. You remember they were coming on vacation here? He's bought Erin a ring but hasn't asked her yet."

"Brave man or very confident."

"I hope it works out for them. This is good. What is it?"

"New Zealand Sauvignon Blanc. Remember, we drank it at that lodge in Haliburton. Speaking of drinking, what do you want to do for dinner?"

"Fish, somewhere."

"I know a place. What else happened today?"

"We went to see Spottiswood. Adam thought it might help if he confirmed my history with them in Vermont, but it didn't. She was as intransigent with him as she's been with me. I feel like a bug trapped in this spider web of an island, and she's the spider."

Thomas hugged her but didn't try to comfort her with any soothing words, and she knew he was as worried as she was.

The restaurant hung suspended over the sea. Lights from somewhere below illuminated an underwater ballet of fish — vibrant reds, oranges, electric blue, peacock green, all sizes and shapes danced in and out of the light and around the coral and feathery plants, all visible through a glassed section of the floor.

"I meant fish to eat, but this is delightful. How did you know it was here?" Anne said.

"Previous trips."

Previous trips. He likely meant when his wife was alive. Although they had talked about her, Thomas almost never referred to their life together. The silence was an obstacle to moving forward in their relationship. She returned to the moment when the waiter arrived, bringing the menu that included, as promised, fish.

"How much longer will you be able to stay?" she asked.

"The meeting is going to be several days longer than we'd planned, and I'll stay until the end, likely after next weekend."

"I changed my flight until next week, if she lets me go then."

"I'm sure it will soon be over."

"She's so stubborn."

"She reminds me a little of Genevieve."

"Genevieve?"

"My wife. She made her mind up very quickly and stuck to it in the face of all opposition and evidence."

"That must have been difficult."

The returning waiter interrupted, and they ordered. "You haven't said much about her, Thomas. I don't know how long you were married or how she died."

"We were married for five years. She developed malignant melanoma in the year our son was born. It was very aggressive, none of the treatments made any difference, and in two months she was gone. She was only twenty-six."

"With Michael, it seems so long ago and so yesterday. But the pain has dulled, or at least when it threatens I can push it down again to where it belongs."

"Yes. I had the children and a very demanding job. My mother helped me and a wonderful woman called Beatrice who still works for me in the New York office did too. After the kids didn't need a nanny, I took her to the office because I saw that she had a genius for organization. I couldn't have done any of it, kids or business, without her."

With a twinge of what she was startled to recognize as jealousy, Anne asked if Beatrice had a family of her own.

"Yes, two boys and a girl. The kids, theirs and mine, were very close and still see each other often. Their dad works for me too."

"You don't like to talk about the past?"

"No, not the emotional past. You?"

"Michael only died five years ago, but no, I don't like to dredge it up, not anymore."

"Don't misunderstand me. It's only my past I don't like to talk about. If you need to talk, if something brings back the pain, I'll listen, and help if I can." Thomas reached across the table to take her hand.

"And if something bothers you, don't keep it to yourself or go all silent on me. I hate guessing," Anne said.

"Deal?"

"Deal."

Chapter Four

Adam called a number he hoped was still in service.

It was answered with hello.

"Jake, Adam Davidson. How's it going?"

"Great. Are you here in Bermuda?"

Adam recognized Jake's voice, but not the accent, somehow changed from African-American to Jamaican.

"Yes."

"Care to meet for a drink?"

"Sure." At least to find out who he was supposed to be.

"And Adam, the name's Quin Randall."

"Where do you want to meet?"

Jake, alias Quin, gave him the name of a bar and how to get there. Adam took a cab from the hotel.

The bar, a whitewashed building, window boxes filled with trailing red geraniums on either side of an open blue door, squatted on a back street in Hamilton. Inside it was just a bar: battered wooden tables, a television playing a sport — soccer, not football — a few sad-eyed men carefully nursing drinks. Quin was sitting on a stool, one eye on the game, the other on the attractive woman wiping down the bar. They shook hands and walked out the back door to a terrace where a few tables huddled in the glare of the sun. Quin sat facing the doors, Adam a collection of wilted potted plants. A woman at another table gave them a brief glance, and then returned to staring, vacant-eyed, into her drink.

"What brings you here?" Quin asked. He shook his head no at the server who brought Adam's beer.

"Vacation. You still posted to the Caribbean?"

"Yeah. Why'd you look me up?"

"Can't I say hello to an old buddy without suspicion. You spooks are all alike."

Now that he was here, Adam wasn't sure Quin was the person he should be talking to.

"Yeah, and you cops are all alike. What's up?"

"A friend of mine is in some trouble here. I'm nosing around a little to see what's going on."

"What kind of trouble?"

"A kid was murdered, and she was there. She's a doctor, and she was trying to help him but the cops her consider "a person of interest"."

"So. What's that got to do with me?"

"So she says the guy she saw murder the kid was also on the plane with her, and later at the estate of a guy called Wainwright and she thought he was checking out the security system there."

"At Wainwright's?" Quin leaned back in his chair and took a long pull at his beer.

"Yeah."

"Fuck." He dropped the bottle on the table with a bang that turned the waiter's head their way.

"Take it easy. Why?"

"High-level stuff, Adam. Can't tell you."

"But somebody checking the security is a problem?"

"Yes. Can I talk to her?"

"If you can find her. I think she's scared and hiding. She has a sister here, but I don't know the name."

"She gave it when she came into the country. I can get that. Does the guy she saw know it?"

"I think likely, yes."

"What do you think she'll do?"

"Dunno. The police don't believe her about the "shark-eyed man" as she calls him, so she might hide. But she's a curious person; she might trying digging into it herself."

"Shark-eyed man. That's how she described him? What else?" Quin leaned forward, his voice dropped, and he sent his eyes around the terrace.

"Six feet, powerful, white hair, pale eyes, square face and a gait she says she can recognize."

"A little hesitation when he walks?"

"Something like that. Can you place him?"

"Yes. She's in bad trouble if he knows she can recognize him. And I gotta go. I also need to talk to her. If you see her, call me."

"Tell me who the guy is?" Adam grabbed Quin's wrist as he stood up.

"No can do, buddy. Thanks for the information." He shook off Adam's hand and strode off. Adam watched him go, drained the last mouthful from his bottle and left.

Erin was sitting in the garden of their bed and breakfast when he arrived back, very late for their lunch. Her dark hair shone in the sunshine, and she was smiling at the antics of the birds, sparrows or something, which flocked to eat the bread crumbs she was dropping for them.

"I'm sorry," he said. "I met an old friend, and we got to talking."

"Who was it?"

"A guy called Quin."

"Does he live in Bermuda?"

"Posted here."

"A soldier?"

"No. One of the agencies. I wanted to talk to him about Anne."

Adam told her that Anne was likely getting herself involved in something major.

"Is there anything you can do?" she asked.

"I don't think so. Do you want to go for a walk after lunch?"

"Yes, let's."

Every day they walked a portion of the Railway Trail, a linear park created from the old Bermuda Railway right-of-way. On a section with the romantic name of Rural Hill to Khyber Pass, where the trail wound through tunnels carved from overhanging trees, he asked her to marry him. She was silent for so long that he was afraid she was trying to say no.

"If you need some time…" he began, holding her in his arms and whispering into her hair.

"I do," she said. "I love you. I want to spend my life with you, but I don't know if can deal with the uncertainty." She looked up into his face, and he saw that she was crying.

"The uncertainty of a cop's life."

"The uncertainty of not knowing what comes first with you, our life together or your job. I know how important your work is to you. Even today, on our vacation, it took you away from me."

"I'll be finished law in two years if I take the full-time option."

"Yes and then you'll join the FBI, and we'll be back into it again. I'm not saying I can't do it, Adam, but now that you've asked and it's more than a dream, I find I have to think a little more. Until tonight. I know I can make a decision, but not with you holding me and loving me."

"I'll hold you forever if it means you'll say yes."

"Let's walk a little."

"Will you wear my ring until you decide?"

"When I put it on, I won't take it off again. You keep it a little while longer."

Chapter Five

Anne decided on a navy skirt, bright pink shirt, her sister's gold chains and black sandals for what Thomas called an "informal lunch". When she finished dressing, she slumped on the bed.

"What is it?" he asked.

"What am I going to do? Between the police and the killer, I see no way out."

"I think you're worrying too much about the police. She can hassle you, but the Director of Public Prosecutions makes the call, not her. As for the other guy, I imagine he's left the island by now. Try to relax and enjoy this afternoon." He reached down and pulled her up into a tight hug.

"I'll try."

The pale yellow house sprawled over what looked to be at least ten thousand square feet. The sun reflected from its whitewashed roof tiles — even the rich of the island collected rainwater. The double-doored entrance of dark cedar opened at the summit of a welcoming arms staircase. Anne wondered if the architect had Bermuda or Versailles in mind when he designed it. The luncheon crowd, easily two hundred people, mingled to the music of a three-piece ensemble, tucked into an alcove.

"No, two-fifty, so I was told," Thomas said when she told him her estimate.

They joined a small group sitting at a table for six near the French doors with a view of the stone-walled terrace. The other guests were two couples from New York, acquaintances of Thomas's.

Lunch was delicious — Bermuda rockfish in a delicate white sauce, young fresh peas and duchesse potatoes. After coffee and lemon soufflé, the members of the working group withdrew, and Wainwright's secretary, a man called John Malcolm, stood up to address the spouses, mostly women, but an occasional man amongst them. Malcolm had met them at the door the previous day. He must be more than a door-opener, Anne decided, taking in his well-cut suit and hearing his polished and confident British speech.

"Ladies and Gentlemen, most spousal programs stuff you into busses and haul you off, quite brutally, to see sights. We offer you the joys of the estate and the golf course. Tennis for those of you who would like to play and we have assorted tennis gear available. For the gardeners amongst you, we suggest a walkabout with our head gardener. For those interested in art, the estate has a collection that would be of some interest. If you want to sit and enjoy the sea and the sun, we can accommodate that as well. I'll be happy to direct you according to what you would like to do."

Anne chose the art tour and started out with two or three others and the young woman guide who was very knowledgeable about the paintings and the artists, particularly the local ones. The group stopped to look at a Corot hanging to the right of the meeting room's door. The security guard moved obligingly to the left; Anne looked towards him to say thanks. The grey eyes of the man from the plane stared back at her. At that moment she knew that he recognized her. The skin of her back crawled with the sensation of being watched, and at the corner of the hallway, she looked back. The guard followed them.

He knew; he knew who she was; he knew that she had seen him at the gallery. Where could she hide? Ahead of her, she saw the jostling, chattering crowd of women who chose to play tennis. The two groups mingled for a moment, and Anne slipped into the midst of those going to change. At the reception desk in the locker area, she picked up a locker key and chose tennis clothes and shoes and a racket. No other way out, she thought. A blank wall surrounded the rows of lockers. Maybe she could blend in with the crowd.

She found her locker, replaced her pink blouse with a white tennis shirt with an alligator on the pocket, pulled her hair up and through the opening in her green ball cap, shoved her wallet and cell phone and gold chains in a pocket of the white shorts and put on her sunglasses.

She saw him watching the exits, but too far away, she hoped, to recognize her in the middle of women all dressed alike.

She was an extra player.

"I'll sit out," she offered and ambled to the furthest court. When she looked back, she saw him moving towards the courts.

She decided to run, away from the house instead of into it.

"I don't know why, " she told Thomas later. "I wanted to get away, and he was between me and the house, and he had that uniform, and no one would pay attention if he said I was an intruder and hustled me away. People here don't believe me."

So she ran, away from the courts and towards the sea. A copse of trees separated the tennis courts from the sea. But it wasn't a beach she saw when she burst through, but the jagged coastline of black rocks and pounding surf. She looked back. He hadn't made it through the trees. She had a moment, just a moment. She groped her way along the rough face of a boulder that balanced on the edge of the cliff. A rudimentary path led between the stone outcroppings. Under one she found a hollow, a sort of cave that widened the further in she crawled. She found enough space to hide at the back of the cave. She turned and brushed away, or so she hoped, the signs of her passage. A wave, higher than the others that splashed in after her, smoothed the sand that formed the floor of the cave. It was enough.

She sat, shielded from the entrance by the turn of the cave wall. The roar and salt-smell of the sea filled the space but didn't drown out the pounding of her heart. She hoped at least she would hear him coming. The sound of her shallow gasping echoed from the stone that surrounded her. Stop it, she warned herself. She'd been in this situation before. She knew panic didn't help but got her in worse trouble. She tried to slow her breathing, to be quiet.

The light in the cave vanished.

Anne tucked in her feet and squeezed as far back into her corner as she could. Light flashed around the cave. But he couldn't crawl in, he was too big, and he didn't see her. After a few moments, he moved on.

She had a new problem. How long to stay in her cave? How high did the sea come? Was it high tide now, or would the sea soon return, filling her cave?

She waited. How long would he search? He had whatever he was supposed to be doing on the estate still to do. Surely he would decide to find her later. It was a small island; how hard would it be to find her? An hour went by. Each successive wave reached further back into the space. The tide was coming in.

She knew she had to go, but where? Thomas would still be at his meeting. Would he look for her at the coffee break? Not likely. He thought she was somewhere, looking at pictures or reading.

She crawled out of the cave and inched her way up the narrow path. If he were still up top, she had no way out.

Chapter Six

Thomas expected Anne to be sitting somewhere, reading, when he didn't find her at their prearranged spot after his meeting, ninety minutes overtime. Even Anne, patient when she was reading a book, might have baulked at ninety minutes. He asked Malcolm if she'd left.

"I don't know where she is," he replied.

"She joined the tennis group, left her clothes in a locker and disappeared."

"Her clothes are still here?"

"Yes. Shall I package them up for you?"

"Yes." Thomas walked away and out the front door. He called their hotel room — no answer — then called Liz. Martin answered.

"Martin, Thomas Beauchamp. Do you know where Anne is or is your mom there?"

"Mom went out. I don't know where."

Thomas went back to his hotel, texted Anne and waited.

She reached the level ground and exploded from behind the

rock, running, away from the estate and along the cliff as far as she could. When she stopped, clutching her side, she found herself on the edge of a golf course. A foursome looked at her, exchanged quizzical glances and then resumed play. She brushed off the seaweed that clung to her wet tennis shorts and shirt and the sand mixed with blood from her scrapped elbows and knees and strolled across the fairway to the clubhouse.

Her phone buzzed in her pocket.

"Hi, I wondered if you would be coming here today," her sister asked. The cheerful voice brought tears of relief to Anne's eyes.

"Can you come and get me? I'm at a golf course called Sheridan's. Can you hurry?"

"I'll be right there."

Twenty minutes later, her sister's car pulled into the circle in front of the clubhouse.

"What happened to you?" Liz asked.

"Later," said Anne.

She climbed into the car and pulled on the seat belt. Her swollen elbow protested, sending pain down into her hand.

"I want to go home, have a shower and get into some clothes that don't stink of fish and seaweed. Don't go straight to your place; make some random turns while I watch behind."

"Why?"

"I'll tell you later. First I have to make sure no one is following us."

"For God's sake, Anne,"

"I don't think I can stay at the hotel or your place."

"What's going on?"

"I saw that man, the one who killed the boy, at the Wainwright's. He was dressed as a security guard, and he recognized me. I changed into these clothes and mingled with the crowd, but he found me and followed me. I hid in a cave in the cliffs and then ran to the golf course."

"Maybe he was a security guard, and you were acting suspiciously."

"Not you too. Liz, he's dangerous. I know he is."

"You know you always make your mind up too quickly about people. Because you didn't like his eyes and he shoved you, suddenly he's a murderer or a terrorist or something. You said you couldn't recognize him."

"He recognized me. You didn't see him and the way he looked at me. The alternative is to go along, trusting that everything will be fine. It's not fine. I have to hide or change my appearance or something. Are you going to help me or not? Where can I stay?"

"Of course I'll help you. My friend's apartment is empty for the next two weeks. I have the key, and she told me my visitors could stay there if they wanted to. But let's stop at my house first so you can have a shower. You don't smell all that great."

Twenty minutes later they were in the car again.

"Can we stop at your hairdresser?"

"Now? Why?"

"I need a cut."

An hour later, Anne's hair was so short her head was covered with tight curls, now dark brown from the temporary rinse the hairdresser applied.

"What do you think? Do you think he would know me?" Anne asked.

"Not unless he was close. Has he heard you talk?"

"Yes."

"How's your French?"

"Good. I could fake an accent in my English and throw in some Italian. Maybe he would mistake me for a European."

"Maybe. Or maybe you could stay in the apartment for the next two weeks until the police are satisfied that you did nothing."

"I don't believe they'll ever let me go."

"Anne," Liz protested," this is Bermuda, not some obscure military dictatorship. We have rights and laws."

"You have rights and laws. Your constitution doesn't apply to visitors."

"I'll ask the lawyer to come to see you. He'll reassure you, I'm sure."

"Maybe. What's the address of your friend's apartment? Do you have the key with you?"

"I can wait."

"No. I need to establish another identity. The room is in Thomas's name, but I have a key. I don't want to risk being seen at the hotel with anyone. Please, Liz. Drop me at a bus stop a block from the hotel, and I'll walk." Anne walked down the long lane, past the main building of the hotel and on down the hill to Thomas's villa. He was lying on the bed when she came in. "Where have you been and what the hell have you done to yourself?"

"I had to. I have to hide." Anne slipped off her shoes and crawled onto the bed beside him, cuddling into his arms while she told him about the cliff and her plan and her sister's objections.

"I agree with Liz. There's no need for all this."

"You haven't seen the way he looks at me." She shook off his arms, climbed out of bed and started pacing the room. "What am I to do? I'm afraid and that woman Spottiswood won't help me. She wants to arrest me. I'm going to stay in that apartment until the conference or whatever it is, is over. I think he's planning something there and he's already killed one man to..."

"To what? What advantage would killing the gardener give him?"

"I don't know. Is there security? There must be. Did he have a passcode? If he was involved with the daughter, maybe he did."

Anne stopped ranting, not wanting to share her sudden thought with Thomas. Her nephew knew the daughter. He could arrange for her to talk with...what was her name? Candice. That's what he'd said. Candice. She started packing.

"If he was all ready inside, why did he need the passcode? Why don't you talk to the lawyer?"

"Maybe he isn't high enough in the security guard business to get a code. Maybe he wants to go in there at night. Maybe he was scoping out the security or the layout of the house. I'll talk to the lawyer, but first I want to get away from anybody he could hurt while he's looking for me."

"You don't know that he's looking for you. He saw you by chance, and you told him you recognized him by running away. But if he doesn't see you again, he won't have to bother about you."

"I'll go for a day or so. If nothing happens, then I can come back."

"What's your sister going to tell Spottiswood?"

"If she comes looking for me, she'll tell her where I am and why I'm hiding."

Anne rode the bus to the apartment she was going to use. It too was part of a larger home that sat high on a hill overlooking the Atlantic. The apartment's front door opened off the driveway. There was no view except the road in front and the neighbor's hedge, but it felt like a safe cave to Anne. She locked the door behind her, took a deep breath and sank into a soft leather armchair.

Okay, now what? She needed to speak to Martin about Candice. She rummaged in her purse for her phone.

"Martin, I need a favor. Can you call me when you have a few minutes?"

Moments late, Martin called back.

"I hate boats," Anne said. She stumbled over the railing in spite of her nephew's helping hand.

"We can talk to Candice privately here," Martin said. "She's below."

"Are we staying here?"

"No. I'm going to take her out. The wind is good. You'd better not talk until we're out there."

"You have an engine as well as the sails, don't you?"

"Yes, but I won't need to use it when we're out on the sea today."

The engine turned over, purred, and moved the boat from its moorings. Anne, caught unawares, lurched down the companionway. She thumped onto a bench and looked up to see Candice staring at her. Candice was the ten-year-old in the picture Anne saw at the Wainwright estate, now all grown up. Or mostly. She was about nineteen, Anne thought. Her blonde hair tumbled over her face. She threw it back in a graceful, casual gesture.

"You must be Martin's aunt," she drawled in the provoking accents of the mid-Atlantic.

"I'm Anne McPhail."

"Why did you want to talk to me?"

"Didn't Martin tell you? He thinks we shouldn't talk until we're out to sea."

"Then I'm going up."

Up sounded good, better than the claustrophobia-inducing cabin. The coastline receded into the blue surrounding the islands and then disappeared. Anne thought they were far enough out, but Martin, picking up a fair wind, allowed the sails to billow and the boat to race across the waves. Candice sat in the bow, making a picture for Martin to look at.

"Aren't we out far enough?" Anne asked.

"Yes. I wanted a short run. Why don't you talk to Candice and I'll head back in a little while. There's weather coming in any way."

He pointed to the horizon where a dark line of clouds threatened the sunshine.

"Oh good."

Anne's stomach, great for trains, planes and automobiles, protested against the roll of the sea. She groped her way to where Candice was sitting.

"I need to talk to you," she said. "Can we go below?"

"I hate it down there when it's so lovely up here. Let's shout."

"I want to know if you gave the code to the estate gates to Nathan Smith."

"Why should I tell you?"

"Because I think he was murdered for it."

"Why?"

"Why was he murdered or why did someone need the code?"

"Why do you think someone needed the code?"

"I saw the man I think murdered him checking your security. What else of value did Nathan have except his knowledge of the estate and that code?"

"You're assuming I gave it to him."

"No, I'm asking. Do you want to ignore the fact that he might have given it or sold it to the murderer? The man took something from his body. Did he write down the code? Come on, Candice. We're talking about your home. Do you want someone to have access to it? Do you want to be responsible for whatever he plans to do?"

Candice started to cry. The wind blew the tears off her face in tiny streams.

"I did love him, you know. And yes I gave him the code, so he could come in at night and see me. No one cares. I couldn't even go to the funeral."

"Who stopped you?"

"The new security detail. They said it wasn't safe. I pretended to go to the gynecologist to get away from them today."

"What's all the security about? Have there been threats against your father?

"No. There's some meeting going on. Not the business meeting. That's a cover. The house is full of Israelis and Palestinians and CIA, and I don't know who else. The important people are coming tomorrow, Dad said. If the storm doesn't get here first."

"Israelis and Palestinians? Both?"

"Yes and a bunch of Americans and some British and all of them pretending to be businessmen."

"There's no actual business meeting going on?"

"I don't think so, although at the big events like the dinner the other night there were some business types, friends of my father."

"I'm thinking you shouldn't be telling me this. Weren't you told not to talk about it?"

"I don't care. Someone killed Nathan, and they brushed it off. Dad ignored it because he has more important things to think about."

Anne felt her heart thumping. She needed to ask the next question, but did she want to know the answer? She wasn't sure.

"Do you know Thomas Beauchamp?"

"Yes, he's one of Dad's friends from New York."

"So not one of the CIA or others?"

"I don't know."

The sunshine disappeared and Anne shivered in a sudden gust of cold wind. She stumbled her way back to Martin.

"Shouldn't we go in?" she said.

"Yes, the storm's coming in fast. Tood won't be happy if I keep her out in it."

"Tood?"

"He owns the boat."

"I won't be happy either, nor will your mother."

"I'll get you back in, Auntie Annie."

"Don't call me Auntie Annie."

She laughed at the childhood name but kept her eyes on the horizon where dark clouds massed.

"What was the marine weather forecast?"

"Clear tonight; storm coming in tomorrow."

"A day early."

"I'll use the engine and get us back in."

The engine turned over once, coughed and gave up with a polite wheeze.

"We'll have to sail her in," Martin said.

"Should you send a distress call?"

"We aren't in distress. Candace and I can sail her."

Martin called to Candace, and they huddled in a discussion, then made mysterious, to Anne, adjustments to the sails. The sea began to roll, and so did Anne's stomach. The dark line of clouds on the horizon drew nearer.

The sea rolled again, and she hit the side to vomit. "Put on a harness," Martin called. He threw one to her and one to Candice. Martin had explained the harness and tether to her on a previous trip, so she knew how to attach it to the boat. The vest would auto-inflate if she hit the water.

No billowing, Anne thought. Shouldn't the sails have been filling with wind?

"There doesn't seem to be much wind to fill those sails," she said.

"This is the Sargasso Sea. The Doldrums. Sometimes no wind for days, until a storm comes up. We'll have wind, and we'll run in front of the storm."

Wind was supposed to make the waves, Anne thought. The waves were rolling the boat and her stomach, but no wind. Martin was waiting, she saw, watching the horizon.

The sails puffed, catching the first breeze. Candice and Martin pulled on ropes, positioning the sails to get the most from the light breeze. Even Anne enjoyed the speed. But the black line of the horizon, now a towering hill of black clouds, engulfed them in driving rain.

Martin at the helm and Candice on the sails struggled to keep the boat, which seemed so big to Anne when she came aboard, upright in the swells that threatened to swamp it. She clung to the rail and struggled to keep from continual vomiting. Martin said the storm would push them home, but she wasn't sure which way that was. She had survived murderous assaults, car and plane crashes and even a previous bout with near-drowning, but this was her lifelong nightmare. She had always been afraid of the sea, of dying in the water.

She looked at Martin's exultant face and realized that to the twenty-two-year-old, this was an adventure. Candice too laughed as she maneuvered the sails. Maybe they weren't going to die, Anne thought. But then, they were only kids. They didn't believe they would ever die

Martin glanced over at her when she hit the side again.

"Auntie Annie, I'll get you home," he reassured her. "Just hang on."

She gave him a weak thumbs-up and turned back to the rail.

Chapter Seven

He walked back along the cliff, looking for signs of the woman. What the hell was she doing, everywhere he went? She didn't seem to be a pro, but she was at the gallery, at the dinner when he made his contact and out here. And she knew him; she was afraid of him, so she must have seen him well enough at the gallery to recognize him.

He finished his shift at the party and rode his motorbike to the hotel. When he reached his room, he called Colette.

"Who is this woman who was at the gallery? The one who tried to save the kid."

"A Canadian doctor. She's visiting her family."

"She's everywhere I go. I'll have to eliminate her if she gets in my way."

"Not necessary. The police have her as a suspect in the murder. It was clever of you to leave the gun behind."

"I took it from a guy in Munich. He'd killed a couple of guys in Turkey so they'll start looking for someone from over there."

"The detective has issues with suspecting native Bermudians of serious crimes."

"That's why she's looking at the doctor?"

"Yes."

"That won't last long. Sooner or later they're going to believe her and start looking for me."

"Our information indicates the detective is very stubborn. You should stop worrying about the doctor."

"Don't tell me what I should worry about. That job is mine, and she's starting to irritate me."

"Remember last time. The controller wants you to stay focused on your job."

"Find out her name and where she is staying."

"The controller won't be pleased."

"Just do it."

He ended the call and poured himself a scotch. It would be satisfying to kill her, after the way she escaped on the cliff. He imagined her laughing at him with her family when she told them the story. He hated being laughed at.

Chapter Eight

He watched the three women stroll down the drive from the house. The gate swung open in front of them and clanged shut behind. Too noisy, he thought. When he left, he'd pick another way out.

He saw two of them, chattering away while they stood at the bus stop. The third wasn't included in the conversation. Not quite one of the girls, he thought and followed her onto a bus.

In Hamilton, she took a back lane up the hill from the main street and turned into a one-story, pink building that housed a tiny cafe. He took off his sunglasses and followed her in.

He sat at the counter and asked for coffee and piece of the rum cake in the countertop display case. The woman joined three others in a booth.

"Hey, Jasmine."

"What a day," she said. "They don't pay me enough to put up with that man."

"Who? The guy what thinks he's a butler?" asked one of the others.

"Yes. Malcolm. Today he cornered me in the pantry. He keeps threatening to charge me with theft if I don't...you know."

"What are you going to do? Quit?"

"I can't quit. I still owe Freddie that thousand. I ain't never going to get out of there."

"Is he after the other girls, too?" The woman who asked the question, a Jamaican girl in her early twenties, leaned towards her.

"They don't have my troubles, and two of them got big men at home. I don't know about Charlene. She don't say much."

"What if you tell the boss? Or the daughter?"

"The boss don't know I exist and the daughter got her own troubles."

"What troubles?"

"Her man got shot at City Hall."

"That was her man?"

"Yeah."

"So what you gonna do?"

"I don't know."

He asked for another piece of cake and more coffee, finished, and ambled outside when the women asked for their bills. He followed Jasmine until she was on a residential street and no one was near.

"Jasmine," he said.

"Who are you?"

She swung around to face him.

"Someone who has the thousand dollars you need."

"Yeah?" She stood with her hands on her hips. "What do I have to do for it?"

"Come sit down a minute." He waved towards a low stone wall. She kept a distance between then when she sat.

"So tell me," she said.

"Get back at the Wainwrights."

"How?"

"I work for a businessman, a guy that Wainwright bulldozed. He wants me to get evidence, but I gotta get onto the estate. I need the code."

"I don't got it. They changed it and only Mary has it."

Good, he thought. She'd do it. Now they only needed to agree on price.

"You see her put it in every day, don't you? Does she have it written down?"

"She has it in a little book. The boss told her to memorize it, but she don't remember numbers."

"Can you get it?"

"When do I get the money?"

"Half now, half when I get the code."

"I have to give the whole thousand to Freddie. I want more than a thousand."

"What do I care? The client's paying. How about a thousand now, and a thousand after?"

"Okay."

At his hotel, he considered the little matter of that annoying woman from the plane. What the hell was she doing at the Wainwrights, and where did she go when she disappeared on the cliffs? He needed a name from the airline. A few minutes later he had it and an address.

"Thanks, Colette."

The motorcycle arranged for him sat in the parking lot of the hotel. He located the address on his phone.

The house sat in the center of a wide lawn that swept down to the road. He parked a few meters up the street and walked down, noting the undefended entrance with its attractive and concealing bushes on either side of a sweeping drive. No trouble getting close to the house, he thought, until he heard the dogs behind a fence that protected the back garden. Cars in the drive, lights shining out from behind pulled drapes and dogs: not the best night for what he had in mind.

Back at the hotel, he poured a drink and sat on the balcony overlooking the harbor. His phone vibrated against his thigh.

"Yes, Colette." He put the phone on speaker, took it back inside and closed the door behind him.

"I've been monitoring traffic on websites in Bermuda. A newspaper is reporting two Maritime Operations incidents. It says that a small craft is becalmed in the Sargasso Sea. The person on board is the subject's nephew and two others. One of them is perhaps the woman in question."

"Is Maritime going after them?"

"They have to finish their current operation: rescuing two Americans whose boat capsized."

"Can you get me a boat?" He drained the last of his drink and waited for the answer.

"Do you need to deal with her before the primary target?"

He snarled into the phone, "Can you get me a boat?"

"Yes, I'll call you back."

A half-hour later he was headed out to sea.

* * *

Lightening flared through the dark clouds, turned them deep-water green and filled the air with the acrid smell of ozone. Wind flapped the sails like bats' wings. The worst was the noise: thunder rolling across the sky, wind whistling and cracking in the rigging, Candice and Martin screaming to each other. Anne fought the wind that ripped at her and sent the waves crashing over the railing.An hour, two — Anne lost track of the time. Then as quickly as the storm hit, it was over. The wind dropped to a whisper; the clouds disappeared; the sun dried the deck and diamond-tipped the waves; the air cleared.

"That was fun," Martin shouted to Candice.

Fun, Anne thought. They called that fun.

"What now?" she asked.

"I'll try to get the engine started."

Candice took the wheel, and he disappeared below. When he reappeared, he shook his head at them.

"Engine won't start, and now there's no wind. I'll see if I can get anyone on the radio."

Anne thought about the Bermuda Triangle. She'd read all the sceptical reports about the so-called disappearances and knew that they'd been debunked years ago. However, becalmed with no engine sounded like a setup for yet another tale.

"No luck with the radio," Martin reported when he came back up.

"So no way to send a distress signal, then?"

"I think there's a satellite phone on board, but Tood hides it in case of looters. Can you help me look?"

Anne followed him down the companionway into the cabin, a cheerful space with red curtains on the windows and yellow and red striped cushions on the benches. Brass pulls marked the drawers and cupboards built into the teak walls. There were two cabins, the forward dedicated to sleeping, and the aft to cooking, eating and sleeping. Martin attacked the drawers, leaving them opened as he finished.

"Would he hide it in an obvious place like a drawer?"

"Maybe not, but he's not a subtle guy."

Perhaps in the oven, she thought. No. A shelf over the stove held only pots, but in the drawer in the base, she found what she hoped was a satellite phone, wrapped in a tea towel.

"Martin, is this it?" she said.

"Yes. Did you see his list of numbers?"

The list was tucked in with other safety equipment. She read Martin the number for Bermuda Maritime Operations.

"Well?"

"They're not happy, especially with the engine failure. We're a long way out. The storm's blown us halfway to Nova Scotia."

"Seriously?"

"No, but we'll have a long wait. See if Tood left any supplies on board, will you?"

No food, but a miniature bar was well equipped, with fruit juice and soda water and tonic as well as alcohol. They took some bottles on deck.

"Should we call our families?" Anne asked.

"Too little power left in the battery. I have to save it in case Maritime wants to reach us again."

"Will Maritime call them?"

"I said there were three of us, two women besides me. They didn't ask any names except mine and Tood's."

"That's relief," Candice said.

A relief, Anne thought. Interesting. Didn't want to worry him or afraid of her dad's reaction? She settled down in a chair on the gently rolling deck and fell asleep. When she woke, she looked over at the wheel where Martin and Candice watched the horizon and lights that

moved steadily towards them.

"That can't be Maritime already," she heard Martin say.

"Should we send up a flare?"

"I'd sooner they missed seeing us. There've been reports of pirates."

"Is this boat much of a prize?" Anne asked.

The boat on the horizon was drawing closer, on a direct course to them.

"No, but Candice might be. Wrap your id in with something heavy and throw it overboard," he suggested.

"I don't want to do that," Candice said. "I want to be able to prove who I am when Maritime gets here."

Chapter Nine

Liz looked up from her book when the car crunched to a stop in front of the house. A tall man, black, with a handsome but guarded face, walked towards her. The face changed with his engaging smile, all bright perfect teeth and crinkled eyes. Must be an American, Liz thought, judging from the teeth. But the accent when he said hello was Jamaican.

"Mrs. Heath, I'm Quin Randall. I wondered if I could talk to you for a few minutes about your sister. May we go inside?"

"No, we'll sit here. Who are you and why do you want to talk to me about my sister?"

Quin dragged a garden chair around to sit opposite her. She sat up straighter, tucked her feet under her chair and folded her arms.

"I work for the American government and I have reason to believe your sister is in danger."

"So does she. Do you have any proof you work for the American government? What branch?"

"I'm in a foreign service. I spoke with Adam Davidson this morning. Do you know him? He's a friend of Anne's."

"I've heard her speak about him, but I don't know him. You'll have to do better than that."

Quin showed her an American identification card that was vague about the department he worked for. Liz studied it for a moment.

"Let's presume you are who you say you are. What do you want with Anne?"

"I want to talk with her about the man she saw at the Wainwright estate."

"The best I can do for you is tell her that. Do you have a number she can call?"

"I'd rather go see her."

"Take it up with her."

He leaned towards her. "Look, there are high-level things happening. I don't have much time, and I have to find her before Blanc does."

"Blanc?"

"We call him that. Started as Great White Shark but the French shortened it to Blanc. Where is she?"

"I don't know."

"Mrs. Heath."

"I don't. She hasn't called me since she went to see my son at the marina."

"Were they going on a boat ride?"

"I don't know but if they did, I don't think Martin intended to be away this long. There's a storm at sea, according to the weather report."

"Are they safe?"

"My son's an experienced sailor, but the boat doesn't belong to him. I don't know."

"Will she come back here, when they get back in?"

"No."

"Give her this when you see her," he said, passing over a business card. "Tell her to call me."

"Telling doesn't work so well with Anne."

"Tell her it's important."

Quin picked up his phone to make a call when he reached his car.

"What the hell's wrong with that woman?" he said when Adam answered.

"Which one?"

"Your friend, Anne. Even her sister doesn't know where she is or what she's doing."

"Or she won't tell you."

"What's all the suspicion about?"

"Anne's having a rough time here and now she can't go home. Liz is protecting her."

"Did you know she went out to sea today?" "I'm surprised. She hates boats."

"Her nephew took her. The sister says there's a storm at sea."

"Did she seem worried?"

"A little, yeah. If you see Anne or hear from her, ask her to call me."

"Will do."

Liz paced from room to room as the day grew longer and still no Martin. At six, Dave came home.

"What's the trouble?" he said when he saw her face.

"Martin took Anne out on Tood's boat. Maritime Operations called. They were caught in that storm and now they're becalmed somewhere on the Sargasso."

"Engine?" Dave was at the computer, reading the marine weather report.

"Not working, nor is the radio. But they have a satellite phone that still had some battery life when they called MO an hour ago.

"Are they going after them?"

"I think so. Can you call?"

Dave's close friend, Ed, was Chief of Maritime Operations, and took his call.

"Sorry to hear Martin's in trouble, Dave. We'll get to him, but we have two Americans in the water about fifty miles out that we have to get to first."

"Do you know if they have any supplies?"

"They have some. We'll get to them, but not soon. He's young; he'll be okay."

"My sister-in-law's with him and she's not that young."

"Health issues?"

"No."

"I'll let you know when we're going out."

"Thanks."

"He says they have to get to two Americans who are in the water first," he said, reporting to Liz on his conversation.

"Damn. Why don't they get into trouble in their own waters. Have you called Tood?"

"No. You know Tood. He'll call or come by if he has anything to say."

Two hours later the ringing phone brought Liz in from the kitchen, dish towel in hand. She watched Dave's face pale.

"Any evidence of whose boat it was?"

Dave listened and then spoke again, "Then the Maria Laura could still be out there? Please call me when you hear anything more."

"What?" Liz said.

"They found evidence of a explosion, pieces of a boat, no one in the water."

"But not for sure? Not the Maria Laura for sure?"

"No, they haven't found anything that identifies the boat."

Liz stepped into his arms and they stumbled together to the sofa. Dave held his head in his hands, and she heard a sob.

"Don't, Dave. Don't. I can't believe they're gone until we have some proof. What if it's not Tood's boat at all? What if they're floating somewhere in a life raft? What if they were kidnapped off that boat? We should call Thomas. Maybe he has more resources." Liz ran her hand over his back; felt the tension in his muscles.

"What kind of resources?"

"I don't know. Satellite or something. But we should call him anyway."

But Thomas wasn't at his hotel. Dave left a message.

The boat drew closer. A strong light pulsed into their eyes and a voice ordered, "Get back from the rail."

"Who the hell are you?" Martin shouted back.

"Someone with a gun trained on you. Make this line fast and back away from the rail."

"And if I won't?"

A shot buried itself in the mast above Martin's head

."Okay, okay." Martin grabbed the line, tied it to the rail and backed away to stand beside Anne and Candice.

Anne gripped Candice's hand when the shooter climbed over the gunwale. It was the face of the man from the plane, who rifled Nathan's dying body, and who chased her along the coast. The eyes were his too — grey and cold and clinical.

"Dump your phones on the deck and all of you into my boat." His weapon moved from one to the other.

"Don't get any ideas about taking off. I can shoot faster than you can start it." He waved the gun at them. "In." A few minutes later he dropped into the boat, motioned Martin to the wheel and pointed to the direction he wanted him to take. Towards Bermuda, Anne hoped. When they were a distance from the Maria Laura, she exploded behind them, sending flame and smoke and noise into the night sky, turning the sea in to one of Turner's battle scenes. She rolled onto her side and slipped into the sea, the fire dying with her.

"Why the hell did you scuttle her? She wasn't even my boat!" Martin yelled.

"Shut up. They'll assume you're dead and won't look for you too hard."

He didn't know her sister, Anne thought. She would never believe that Anne or Martin were dead until she saw the bodies.

Two hours later they reached a small island offshore where a yacht loomed beside a pier. Blanc herded them off the smaller boat and up the ramp to the larger one, down into the living area and into a forward cabin. He forced Candice to tie Martin and Anne around their wrists and then tied her.

"I'll be back," he said.

"Wait," said Candice. "I have to go to the bathroom."

"Too bad." He slammed the door behind him. Anne heard the lock fall into place.

Chuck Wainwright loomed over the two men from the security men detailed to watch Candice. "How long has she been missing?'

"Coming up to four hours, sir. She told us she had a gynecologist's appointment and didn't want us sitting among the mothers and other women. You know doctors' appointments. They take a long time. When we thought it was long enough, we went in and they said she hadn't been there. We searched the area and called some of her friends and then came back here."

"Four hours. So you're saying she did this disappearing act herself."

"Looks that way."

"Get out."

When they left he sat down at his desk and called Quin Randall. His leg brushed a holster attached to the side of the desk kneehole. The feel of the smooth leather always reassured him. He'd bought the gun and hidden it there when he started to receive death threats from antigun nuts. He could protect himself, but he'd always kept security around Candice. He thought he could keep her safe. He thought she understood.

Thomas and Quin walked into the room behind Malcolm.

"What's going on?" Quin asked when the butler left the room.

"My daughter's missing. She apparently gave the security guards the slip and they didn't tell me for four goddamn hours."

"How?'

"It doesn't matter. She did and she hasn't come home."

"Any idea where she might have gone?" Thomas asked.

"No. I'll call her maid. She might have told her."

He spoke into the phone and few moments later a slim dark woman came in.

"Cousins, do you know where Candice was going today?"

"She didn't tell me, no, sir." The soft Jamaican voice hesitated.

"What do you suspect?" Thomas asked.

"I think she went on a boat. She took her shoes she wears on boats and her sailing jacket."

Quin dialed Maritime Operations.

"Okay, thanks," he said and then turned to the others. "Maritime is reporting an explosion on a boat that called for help earlier in the afternoon. There's not much left. Not enough to identify for sure. No survivors in
    the water."

"Did they say what boat?"

"She's called the Maria Laura. Dave Heath's son took her out this afternoon." He turned to Thomas.

"I'm sorry, Tom, but two women, one they think his aunt, were with him."

"Can you get satellite?"

"I can try."

Thomas slumped in one of the armchairs across from Wainwright and listened to Quin call in favors. Time passed. Coffee, brought in by Malcolm, cooled in front of Thomas and Wainwright. Quin drank cup after cup, waiting for his callbacks.

"Okay, thanks." Quin pocketed his phone and turned to the others.

"This is what they saw. About three hours ago, a pass over that part of the Atlantic started. The footage shows a small boat racing away from the Maria Laura. They can see the name on the hull. A few minutes later, when the other boat is out of range, she explodes and sinks."

"Scuttled. Did they see who was in the other boat?" Thomas asked.

"No, but they counted at least four people."

"Four. So they were kidnapped?" Wainwright said.

"Looks like it. I'm sorry."

"You and your goddamn fucking meeting."

"We'll have to let the police know."

"I think we should wait until we have something to tell them, like a ransom demand. They're looking for them anyway," Quin said.

Wainwright started shouting again about the meeting endangering his family.

"They're only looking out at sea," Thomas said. "I'd better call Anne's sister."

He left the yelling behind and called when he was in the hall.

Dave answered the phone.

"Dave, Thomas Beauchamp. I wanted to tell you that we've received word from an American source that at a boat with at least four people on it pulled away from the Maria Laura, before she went down. So we think they're still alive."

"Any ransom demand?"

"No, none here. You?"

"No."

Dave hung up and turned to Liz.

"Thomas has information they were taken off the Maria Laura. So maybe they want money."

"Money? Why would anyone target us?"

"Not us. The Wainwright girl was with them."

"Why?"

"I don't know."

～

"Any point in yelling?" Anne asked.

"I don't think so," Martin said. "There's nothing on this island except the pier. Some American guy owns it and can't get permission to build, so he parks his boat here when he's in Bermuda."

"This man, you mean?"

"No. The man who owns it is an older guy."

Anne sat on the edge of the only chair. Her arms began to ache from being tied behind her back. Martin moved towards a narrow door, and leaned on the levered door handle. He stumbled into the room beyond when the door swung open. Anne could hear him swearing.

"What is it?" she called.

"The head. I'm going to look for something to cut these ties."

Candice followed Martin in and asked him for some privacy.

"You're joking. How are you going to manage?"

"I'll manage. Out."

Martin sat on the bed, beside Anne's chair. "I'm sorry, Auntie Annie."

"It's not your fault, Martin."

"I should have had a gun. Tood never goes out without a weapon."

"And what would have happened? This guy is a pro. You saw how he was able to shoot around you. If you had a gun, he would have killed you, and maybe all of us. Guns only bring trouble to the people who own them. And what if you killed him? There you would be, forever a person who killed someone. That's not easy to live with, Martin."

"I know how you feel about guns, but what's going to happen to us? What if he's waiting to kill us?"

"He's a pro. He has a reason to keep us alive, as hostages or for ransom, or something."

"Martin, come here. I found some nail scissors but I can't reach them," Candice called.

Cutting the ties that held Martin's hands took what seemed to be hours. Anne and Candice took turns with the scissors, nibbling away at the plastic and Martin's wrists and their own fingers. When his hands were free, he cut the other two. Anne sat rubbing her shoulders and elbows, trying to get some circulation back.

"What now?" Candice asked.

"We'll have find a way out," said Anne.

"If you can break the scissors apart, I can pick the lock," Candice said.

"Where did you learn that?" Anne asked.

"A boyfriend."

It took her only a few moments and then they were out of the room and out on the pier.

"We need a way off the island, Martin. Is it too far to swim?"

"Yes. There should be an inflatable on a boat this size." He pulled up a flat panel on the foredeck to reveal tools and a small motor. Another panel beside it held a raft that inflated when he pulled it from the storage unit. Candice and Martin dragged it to the railing and over onto the dock and then into the sea. Martin attached the motor and threw in the paddles and other equipment.

"Hurry, Martin. I hear a boat," Anne urged.

Chapter Ten

When he arrived back at his hotel, Blanc called Colette.

"What have you done?"

"Taken out a little insurance. I found those three on the water and took them. They're secure on the yacht for the time being, but I'll have to move them to somewhere on land."

"I'll speak to the controller. He will not be pleased."

"My job, my rules."

"I'll tell him that, shall I?"

"Colette."

"I'll get back to you with a change in location."

He poured a drink, sat on the balcony and waited. Colette was getting difficult. He would have to discuss that with the controller when the job was over; maybe suggest a man, not a goddamn woman next time.

"I've sent the coordinates to your phone. The controller will arrange to leave the key for you. I've sent instructions about that as well. He is not pleased. You know he wants no trail from you to him. That is why you were supposed to get the code yourself. And that is why he is very annoyed at having to leave the key for you now."

"Don't want to hear it, Colette. I'm the one taking risks."

"Don't kill them."

"Good-bye, Colette."

Back on his boat, he could see the yacht ahead of him in the dusk, and the bright yellow life raft being launched from the dock. He'd get there before they were all in the raft, but if one got away, he was done. He fired on the raft and watched them scramble onto the dock and run towards the land. He fired shots into the ground ahead of them and when they stopped, drew along side.

"Get in."

"What do you want with us? Why are you doing this? If you want money, my father will pay. Call him. Call him." Anne reached for Candice's hand.

"Shut up. You," he said, pointing to Anne, "get in and keep her quiet."

He motored slowly around the islands, dropped anchor in the shallow water of a secluded bay and ordered them over the side. Once on shore, he herded them up towards the hulking dark mass of a building.

"What's this?" Anne whispered to Martin. "Shut up," Blanc ordered.

They struggled in silence through the sand to the rocky cliff and up stairs rough-hewn into the hillside that ended at a padlocked door, blocked by sand pushed against it by the wind. Blanc turned a key in the padlock— no noise, no grate of protesting metal — and opened the door to a black deeper than that of the moonless beach behind them.

"In," he said. Anne stumbled into Martin from the blow to her back, a parting shove from Blanc. They both went down. The door behind them closed; the padlock clanged; the only sound was Candice's sobbing.

"Are you okay, Anne? Candice."

"I'm okay. Where are we?" Anne said.

"What are we going to do?" Candice said.

"We're in the old shoe factory. You remember, Candice. The one along the beach from your place that all the fight was about."

"Fight?" Anne asked.

"Yeah, some ownership thing. It was supposed to be torn down or recycled or something but the case has been in court for years. We played here when we were younger."

"Inside?"

"Sure, all over."

"Do you know where we are now?"

"That was the sea door. Someone put a new lock on since the last time I was here. We're in a corridor that goes to the factory floor."

"Is there a stair or a door between us and the floor?"

"Yes. Both. I can get us out if he hasn't barricaded the door at the end of the corridor."

"Or even if he has. Remember, Martin. There's a tunnel that leads back up to the manager's house. I think we could still get through." Candice's words tumbled out and the hand holding Anne's squeezed tighter.

"Or maybe you could anyway," Martin said. "You're the thinnest."

"I couldn't go alone in the dark. I couldn't."

"Let's find the door first," Anne said.

"Watch for debris. Go slow," Martin said. "They haven't cleaned up in here for years. Stay near the walls. We need to hold onto each other."

The fetid air smelled of rats and decay and salt. Damp slicked the walls. They stumbled over the detritus left behind when humans abandon a dwelling to the rodents.

"Damn," said Martin.

Anne and Candice piled up behind him at the door to the factory floor.

"Locked?"

"I don't know yet."

Anne heard a faint whisper — Martin running his hands over the door, seeking its handle.

"There's a heavy lock. We'll have to find that tunnel."

"Do you remember where it is?"

"Halfway back on the right, low on the wall."

They crept back, hugging the wall, feeling for the opening with each step. Anne wiped the slime from her hands off on her jeans.

"Here it is. The tunnel's wider than I remember." Martin said. "I think I can go first. If I can make it all the way along, you can too."

"Don't make me go last," Candice pleaded.

Anne crawled into the narrow space, felt the door and shoved it closed with her foot before she moved to catch up with Candice. Behind her, she heard a muffled metallic clang.

"I think he's back," she whispered.

"Keep moving," Martin said. "Did you close the door to the tunnel."

"Yes."

Anne strangled a cry as Candice's foot caught her nose. She tasted the salt of the blood dripping into her mouth. She scrubbed at her face with her hand and crept on.

"How far?" Anne whispered.

"Not too far now," Candice said.

Anne felt her way through the sludge that coated the floor of the tunnel, heard the scurry of tiny feet and gagged when the rodent smell hit her throat. Her hand touched something that wasn't the floor or the wall, more like a case or a box with a handle. Her hand closed over it, and she dragged it with her.

"Candice," Martin said. "There's a branch here that I don't remember. Which way to the house?"

"Go left. The other one leads out to the sea wall."

"Does someone live in the house?"

"I don't know," Martin said. "But the tunnel ends outside, behind an old shed, if they haven't filled it in. I think we can stand up now. There was always more room at the entrance."

"Hurry, before he finds the tunnel," Candice urged. "We're here. The way out is up a few steps, three I think, and then a trapdoor."

The rotting planks in the door dropped dust and dirt into their upturned faces. The darkness seemed as thick as that behind them.

"Are you sure we're outside?" Candice asked.

"Yes, I can smell the sea," Martin answered.

The trapdoor opened behind a building, not the factory according to Martin, but a shed that held the gardener's tools. They huddled behind it, shielded from the factory. Anne could hear the distant sounds of doors slamming and then a boat revving.

"Maybe he's gone," Candice whispered.

"We can't count on that. Where to from here?" Anne said.

"I think we should try to make it to Candice's house.

There's security there."

"We'll have to go along the shore in case he's watching the roads," Candice said.

"Or he's watching the shore because that's also the quickest," Martin said. "If he's still there."

"Pick one," Anne said, "before he finds the tunnel."

"How could he find it? You have to know it's there," Martin said.

"How did he find us, in the middle of the ocean? Who knows who he is or why he's here? Let's go."

Martin pointed back towards the sea and took a faint pathway sketched through the trees. Candice and then Anne followed. Anne still clung to the case she'd found in the tunnel.

Martin and Candice walked sure-footed along the path that followed the coastline and down through the rocks that loomed above a cove. Anne recognized the cave opening and knew they were behind Candice's home. The gardens were in darkness, but lights flickered through the trees from the house beyond.

"The security will be on," Candice said. "We'll set it off as soon as we climb the path."

"Good," Anne said. "Then we'll be safe."

A horn wailed; lights flared, illuminating the grounds; men

rushed from the house towards the sea, drawing weapons and yelling at them to get down.

"I will not. This is my house," Candice yelled back. "Get down before someone shoots you," Martin said.

He yanked on her arm to take her with him to the ground.

The guards hauled them up and shoved them towards the house. Candice's father appeared in the doorway.

"What are you doing? Take your hands off my daughter!

"We didn't know—" one guard began.

"Save it," he ordered. Candice collapsed against him, sobbing and babbling about the explosion and the kidnapper.

"Bring them into the library."

They marched past a row of shocked faces—the guests at the conference—into a book-lined room. One of the guests spoke to a staff member and walked down the corridor to another door of the library.

"Chuck, I'd think I'd better join you," Thomas said. He crossed to Anne, who stood, holding Martin's arm and staring down the security detail.

"What happened?" he asked Anne.

"The man from the gallery happened. He kidnapped us from the boat, and sank it and locked us in an old building. The old shoe factory, Martin said it was. Martin and Candice knew a tunnel out of it and here we are."

"What did he want?"

"He didn't say. Do you think they'll believe me now? Was there any ransom demand?"

"No," said Wainwright.

"Then he wanted us for something else, hostages maybe. He never said anything to us to suggest he knew who Candice was, but he recognized me. He found us in the middle of the Sargasso Sea, so he must have help, an organization behind him. I don't know what you people are doing here, but I think he's a threat."

Wainwright started to say something, but Thomas broke in, "I need a word."

He walked with Wainwright to the other end of the room.

That was odd, Anne thought. What could Thomas have to say that would matter? But when Thomas returned he didn't explain, but took Anne and Martin to a car and home.

Chapter Eleven

Adrienne rang the doorbell of the Heath home. Behind her she heard a bike stop on the street and then drive on. Dave Heath opened the door.

"I'd like to speak to Doctor McPhail, please."

"I'm sorry. If you know what she's been through today, you must know she needs rest."

"I have to speak to her. If I need to arrest her for trying to escape the island, I will."

"My son took her for a sail, and they were caught in that storm this afternoon. No escaping going on. You'll have to wait until I call the solicitor."

"I'll do that."

"In your car."

"Don't be ridiculous."

"You're not coming into my house until the lawyer arrives."

He shut the door in her face. The solicitor arrived a long twenty minutes later.

"Your client needs to make herself available for questioning," she said.

"Good evening to you, too, Deputy-Inspector. She is, at all reasonable times and hours. What brings you here tonight?"

"She tried to escape from the island."

"Come off it, Adrienne. Escape? In a borrowed boat, with her nephew and Chuck Wainwright's daughter on board? Kidnapped, the boat blown up—what more do you want?"

"She panicked, and she arranged the so-called kidnapping."

Why, she thought, does everyone believe this woman? Nothing easier than for her to toss the gun out the door, and start C.P.R..

"Try that before a judge. What do you want?"

"The truth."

"You've been told the truth. Try looking for the actual murderer."

"I believe your client killed that boy."

"Why? A boy she didn't know, hours after she'd arrived on the island. No motive, Adrienne. No motive."

"Bring her in tomorrow morning."

"I'll let you know."

Dave brought Ken into the living room.

"Thanks for coming, Ken," Anne said. "This is my friend Thomas Beauchamp." After they shook hands, she continued, "I'd like him to be with us while we talk."

"If you want. Let's go to the library."

The library, a square room, lined on two sides with mahogany bookshelves and the other two with French windows, overlooked the gardens that surrounded the house. Reading lamps created circles of light around comfortable chairs facing the fireplace.

"Sit down, please." Anne waved a hand towards the chairs. Thomas sat back near a desk in one corner.

"She seems to believe that you killed that boy." The blunt statement, delivered in a dry, matter-of-fact lawyer's tone felt like a blow. Tears hung behind her eyelids; she forced herself to be calm, but her voice shook.

"Why?"

"Stubborn, I think. She decided on you at first sight and won't give you up easily. You were there; you're not Bermudian; you won't be compliant with her every demand."

"What can we do?"

"Find an alternative."

"I gave her one, and she doesn't believe me. Adam talked to her, and that made her angrier."

"Adam?" He jotted the name down on the legal pad he pulled from his briefcase.

"Adam Davidson, an American policeman that I worked with on those two cases in Vermont. He's here on vacation."

"Would he testify?"

"Of course. So would his boss."

Thomas spoke up. "Character witnesses aren't likely to stop Spottiswood."

"What do you suggest?"

"I have a few contacts who have friends at the top of the government here. Let me talk to them."

"Spottiswood won't like that."

"Anything that gets me off this island is fine by me," Anne said. "And if influence is what it takes, then influence it is. Why doesn't she believe what Martin and Candace told her?"

"Martin is your nephew, and Candice is well-known for flouting authority. You can when you're as rich as her father is. Do what you can, Thomas," he said.

Anne walked out with the lawyer, and, after he left, down to the water's edge and out to the end of the dock to where Dave moored his boat. Across the Sound, she could see the lights of the city winking at her. She turned back. Thomas stood at the end of the drive, waiting. He was afraid, she thought. He wouldn't have suggested he speak to someone influential if he hadn't thought this would end badly. When she came up to him, she asked, "Thomas, what do you know that I should know? Why are you so worried?"

"You were abducted, and now a police officer thinks she should be arresting the victim. Why wouldn't I be worried?"

"It's more than that, isn't it? What's going on at the Wainwright estate?"

"I can't tell you. It's a security issue, and I took an oath."

"An oath. When are we, the Middle Ages? These secrets are going to get me killed, or jailed, and I won't even know why." She swept by him into the house, whispered to her sister, and came out again to climb into Liz's car.

"Where are you going?" Thomas asked.

"Back to my hole, to hide until this is cleared up. If you want to talk to me, call Liz."

Chapter Twelve

B lanc found a message from Colette waiting for him at his hotel. Call immediately, it read.

"They are not happy," she said. "Why?"

"You are taking too many risks in trying to eliminate this woman. Focus on the conference and what you have to do. Now the police will be looking for them and you."

"Not for them. They escaped."

"It gets better and better, doesn't it? What now?"

"I'm getting the access code for the Wainwright estate tonight, and I'll go in as soon as the target arrives."

"Did you not kill the boy to get that code?"

"They keep changing it. Someone is suspicious."

"Or cautious. You would do better to try that as well."

"It would be better if we could get the information from the inside. Why not?"

"His call. He wants no suspicion to fall on himself."

"What's the schedule?"

"Not confirmed. I will get back to you when it is. Stay focused."

He arranged to meet Jasmine on the Railway Trail near his hotel. The trail wasn't all that secure, but it was late, and perhaps it would be quiet at midnight. At the entrance to the tunnel, he could see her white summer dress shining in the moonlight.

"Did you get it?" He walked past her.

"Do you have the money?" The sound of her footsteps followed him deeper into the tunnel.

"Stop," she called. "I'm not going in there, in the dark."

"Show me the code."

"Here's half of it." She passed him a note.

He gave her five hundred dollars in exchange. She turned away from him and tucked it inside her dress. She handed him another note with the final numbers scrawled in pencil.

"Did she see you take it?"

"No. I did it while she were changing. Where's the rest of my money?"

He handed her the roll of bills and waited for her to turn away to count it and then hide it. He took a thin cord from his pocket, ran his fingers lightly over it and then looped it over her head and tightened it around her neck. She was strong, and struggled against the cord, kicked back at him and tried to pry it from her neck. Only a few seconds and the struggle stopped. He knotted the cord, ending it with a precise bow. He reached inside her dress, brushing past the still-warm breasts to retrieve his money.

He walked the few blocks down to the sea, took off his shoes and changed to the ones in his backpack. He threw the ones he'd been wearing into the sea. The rising tide would obliterate his prints.

Chapter Thirteen

The first rays of the sun rising over the sea wakened Adam and drew him out of the room where Erin still slept. He dressed in his running gear, tan shorts and a University of Vermont tee shirt, scribbled a note and left it propped on the coffee-maker.

An entrance to the railway trail was only a few blocks away. He ran into an unlit tunnel, the longest one on the route. In the dim light near the exit, he saw an indistinct bundle lying along the side that grew to be a body as he ran closer.

A small dark woman, her face suffused with blood and her eyes and tongue protruding, a thin cord tight around her throat, lay with her head towards the light. Did the killer catch her when she was running away or did she walk into the tunnel with him? Not his business, he remembered.

He stood beside the body, waiting for the police to arrive, directing joggers and walkers to turn back. The first on the scene were uniformed, but the trim, pant- suited figure of Adrienne Spottiswood soon stalked in and stood looking down at the body and then up at Adam.

"Lieutenant Davidson. You and your friends are making a habit of this."

"This?"

"Finding bodies. Do you now who she is?"

"No."

"Could you wait outside?"

"Yes."

Adam went, called Erin and told her what was going on. A few minutes later, Adrienne came up to him.

"Her name was Jasmine Lawrence. Does that mean anything to you?"

"Not a thing."

"She worked on the Wainwright estate."

"Something important going on out there?"

"Why do you ask?"

"Two bodies associated with the place. Worth a question or two, I'd say."

"Yes, questions for your friend, Doctor McPhail."

"Don't you ever quit? You'll never find your killer if you keep focusing on Anne. I know her, and she's not a killer. She's also very astute and could help you if you'd let her. You need to be looking for the man who kidnapped her."

"If she was kidnapped."

"I suggest you talk to the CIA operative here."

"There's no CIA operative on Bermuda."

"You're not too far up the food chain, are you? Ask your boss. If you don't need me anymore, I'm leaving."

"Don't go too far," she called to his retreating back.

Adam slowed his pace and settled into a walk when he reached the road that led to their bed and breakfast. He sat on the low wall that surrounded the pink and white house and called Quin.

"I found another body, a maid at the Wainwright estate and I thought you should know. Whatever is happening out there, the body count is rising."

"Blanc."

"This one was strangled. I think she might have arranged to meet him. What could she have that he might want?"

"Security code, maybe. I'll bet he didn't count on us getting involved so soon. We'll change it again."

"I suggested the detective call the CIA operative and she threw a fit, claiming there was no CIA on the island."

"Ha. She hasn't been told about the meeting."

"Can you protect Anne from her?"

"Not yet."

"Damn."

Adam dialed again, this time his boss in Vermont. The phone call over, he walked into the house and found Erin sitting at a table on the terrace. He sat down across from her and reached for her hand to touch the ring that by some miracle she still wore.

"Will we be able to go home tomorrow?" she asked. Adam reached across and took off her sunglasses. Her eyes, red-rimmed and swollen, told him she'd been crying.

"I'm so sorry."

"It's not your fault some maniac is loose on this island."

"Yes, we'll be able to go home tomorrow. I called Jim. He'll call the Chief here and tell him that he needs me back home."

"Won't that woman, that detective, hold you as a material witness or suspect or something, the way she did Anne?"

"No. Brother cops aren't treated that way."

"For once I'm glad there's a network."

"Let's go have some lunch."

An hour later they were relaxing over their desserts. Erin fell quiet watching the birds swooping and diving over the water. In the silence, he heard fragments of the conversation at the table behind him.

"What's happening out at Wainwright's?"

"High-level international government meeting, I think, although they're all supposed to be businessmen."

"Why?"

"Why the meeting? I don't know."

"No, why do you think that?"

The voices fell, Erin said something about the birds, and when Adam could hear again he picked up the words "...Israeli at that table across the room, supposed to be a businessman."

"What is he?"

"I knew a guy who looked like him in London. He was Mossad."

"Are you certain?"

"No, but fairly sure."

"You going to mention it to anyone?"

"Not my business."

Adam told Erin he was going to the washroom and walked towards the interior of the restaurant. He passed the table with the lone patron—a blond, blue-eyed giant. Not your typical Israeli, Adam thought. But who knew? When he got back, all the men were gone, and Erin sat alone on the terrace. His heart turned over when she turned her head and smiled at him.

"Let's pack," she said, "and go for one last walk on the beach."

Chapter Fourteen

A small blue car left its parking spot further along the road and eased into the traffic behind Liz. Paula stopped uphill from the house and waited. When she thought Anne was alone, she walked down past houses with closed drapes and quiet front laws. No one home here, she thought. Great place to hide.

Two numbers marked the house, 7 and 7-A. She guessed that Anne was in the apartment and knocked.

"Yes."

The voice came through the door.

"I'm Paula Benson of the Bermuda Reporter. I'd like to ask you a few questions about the death of Nathan Smith."

"I'd rather not. Please leave."

"I'll have to visit your sister and her family instead." The door swung wide, and Anne stepped aside for Paula to enter.

"Thanks, Doctor McPhail."

"Don't thank me yet. What can I possibly tell you that is more than the story in the Gazette this morning?"

"You could start by telling me why you are hiding."

"Because someone's trying to kill me. Now I'll have to move again, thanks to you."

"Who?"

"The man who killed Nathan."

"What does he look like?"

"You can't expect me to tell you that."

"I could help flush him out."

"Or give him another reason to kill me."

"All I want is a little first-person story."

"No. Go." Anne slammed the door behind Paula.

Paula sat in her car while she phoned her paper. "S
orry Paula. We can't print that. The police gave me a call to ask
that we keep her location quiet for now."

"Spineless jerk, she thought.

"What? Since when do we do what the police tell us?"

"Just come back to the office."

Blanc eased up on the motorcycle to follow the little blue car
and the one ahead of her. Who was she and why was she following
the McPhail woman? Perhaps the controller made another arrange-
ment to take care of her? He called Colette.

"Yes."

"I have a car registration number for you."

He rattled off the numbers.

"Just a moment."

"That car is registered to Paula Benson, a reporter for a new
publication, The Bermuda Reporter."

"Can you hack her cell? I want to know everything that has to
do with McPhail."

"Yes, but—"

"Just do it."

Moments later his phone buzzed in his ear.

"Yes."

"A little more information. This woman is English and seems to
be friends with the investigating officer, Spottiswood."

He followed the car and the one ahead of it, until he saw
Anne get out and start up the hill. He'd let the reporter get the

information he needed and come back for the interfering doctor later.

Late that evening he picked up another call from Colette.

"She is staying in the apartment attached to the house at number 7. The owners are friends of her sister and away."

Useful, that reporter and chatty on her non-secure phone.

Anne pulled the door shut behind her, turned the deadbolt, sank down onto the sofa, closed her eyes and willed herself to relax. Her first thought was about her hair. She cut and dyed it for nothing. That man, Blanc, knew what she looked like and would come after her again. She knew she couldn't stay, sitting and thinking in that claustrophobia-inducing space until that idiot woman published where she was, or Blanc found her or the police came for her. She needed some work to do.

She carried the case she'd found in the tunnel to the table in the kitchen, sat on one of the red and white striped chairs and inspected the lock. It was a new- looking combination type, out of character with the battered, salt-stained leather of the case itself.

No way to open the lock but the hinges looked less daunting. She found a tool in the kitchen, the kind with multiple screwdrivers. One of the heads fit the screws on the hinge.

The case held two files and a disk—one file labeled Roberts and the other Wainwright. The disk was anonymous.

The Roberts file contained all the letters that Margaret Smith had written: to the government; to the Archive and Wainwright himself. Most were pleading but the most recent accused Wainwright of killing her son. The other file held the replies, growing irritable as the letter frequency increased, the last threatening legal action of Margaret didn't stop harassing him. In neither file did Anne find any documents that might prove Margaret's claim.

She'd packed her laptop when she moved from Liz's home. She

inserted the disk. Photocopies of land conveyances and mortgage records back to the early twenties seemed to show that Wainwright at least purchased in good faith. Bermuda didn't have a system of recording land transfers in the way that Canada and other nations had. Someone went to a great deal of trouble to research every document related to the Tucker's Town property. If it were Nathan's work, he was a far better researcher than his mother knew.

A notation dated 1928 stated that the owner, Noah Roberts, refused the money offered when the others were selling out. Eventually, an expropriation letter arrived, and he was moved. How reluctantly, she wondered. Did the police drag him from his home, in front of the demolition crew? Newspaper files might tell her, if she could find them and if the relevant issues hadn't crumbled to dust. She would go to the newspaper or the Archive, but first, she needed sleep.

When she awoke, it was late in the morning. Time to change her appearance again.

Two hours later she was blond once more, her hair tucked under a floppy yellow hat, and huge sunglasses hiding most of her face—the best she could do from the neighborhood store at the end of the lane.

She rode a bus into Hamilton but got off a few stops before the main terminal, walked past the City Hall and turned right in Par-La-Ville Road and up to the Royal Gazette building at number 2 on the opposite side of the street. She stood for a moment, watching, then crossed.

The receptionist told her that the Bermuda National Library housed the archive, in a building near the post office in the next street.

Out on the street, she felt an icy chill tighten the muscles of her back, a feeling of being watched. She hurried downhill and turned left through a moon gate—the oldest one in Bermuda, she remembere—and on across the park. Workers from the adjoining Government buildings eating lunch; a father carrying a baby on his shoulder; young mothers strolling with carriages, engaged in happy conversation; an occasional stray tourist shooting photos of the fish pond and the flowers: all mingled in the sunshine, enjoying the tranquillity and beauty of the park. Anne sped along the red stone paths, still with the feeling she was being watched or followed and left through the gate next to the Post Office. She stepped inside, then watched the park exit for anyone who might be following her.

He stood the motorcycle against the curb in front of the house Anne was staying in. A knock at the door went unanswered. Afraid or absent. Next door a woman was weeding a garden thick with flowers. Two kids sat on the porch, intent on licking chocolate ice cream from their fingers and dripping cones.

She looked up at him and got to her feet.

"Good morning," he said, smiling what he hoped was a reassuring smile.

The woman brushed the dirt off her hands and glanced back at her children.

"Good morning."

"I need some help with directions. I was supposed to meet my friend, a woman with short dark hair, here at number 7, but there's no one home."

"There was a woman staying in 7 A, but she's gone away."

"You're certain?"

"She left. That's all I know."

"Did you kids see her come back?" he called over to the porch.

The two heads shook no. "Thanks."

"If she comes back, do you want me to tell her you were looking for her?"

"No. I want to surprise her. I'll be back."

The two-story, square white building was Bermuda's oldest post office and still functioned as a branch. The interior, refurbished and furnished in the simple style of the original postmaster, shone with polished Bermuda cedar counters and beams. Anne stood inside the door watching the exit from the park and the motorcycle stand in front of the building. One man, who stood out from the others because he'd put on his black and red helmet while still in the park, started to rearrange items in his motorcycle saddlebags. He scanned the street and then focused on the post office.

Anne whispered to the woman behind the wicket," Do you have a washroom I could use? I'm afraid I'm going to be sick."

"Certainly, love. Come this way."

Anne slipped inside as the helmeted man entered.

She didn't think he'd seen her.

She stayed inside as long as she dared, hoping the cheerful post-mistress hadn't mentioned her, hoping the man hadn't gone on to search the Library and Museum next door.

The Bermuda National Library, another two-story building, modern, yellow with black shutters, stood back from the street in a garden resplendent with palms and flowering shrubs. Anne walked past the adjoining museum. As promised, the Reference library on the main floor held microfilmed copies of the Bermuda Recorder and the Royal Gazette, for the years of the expropriation. With the librarian's help, she found the story of Noah Roberts and his doomed fight to hold onto his home.

He and his family were dragged from their home, in front of the demolition crew. The developer's nephew signed the order-in-council that allowed the takeover, according to one enraged letter to the editor, but on the whole, there seemed to have been popular support for building the private enclave that was a second home to many of the foreign wealthy. The American tourist dollar was welcome then as now. Anne wondered if an injustice done so long ago could be addressed in the courts here as native rights in Canada were. At the very least, the current owner might have to fight a nuisance suit and its nasty publicity.

Someone took it seriously enough to record the information and hide it in the briefcase in that fetid tunnel. Why the tunnel, she wondered. Who would think a tunnel more secure than a bank or a lawyer's office? Perhaps someone who didn't have access to banks or lawyers, someone like Nathan Smith.

The microfilm reader she was using sat in front on one of the lofty windows overlooking the front courtyard. When she looked up from the dizzying perusal of newspaper pages, she found herself watching Blanc. She ducked behind the reader and then scurried across the room to the stairs to the second floor. Past them, she saw a fire exit. She pushed out, triggering an alarm and outraged yells from the librarian. The park lay ahead, and she ran.

The path, surfaced with flat stones, turned and ahead of her rose a short flight of steps leading into an area of broad borders, lush with flowering shrubs. Dense flowering shrubs, she thought, and stepped around one to find the narrow gravel path she expected, a maintenance access for the gardeners. She followed it along to the widest, thickest shrub, fragrant with crimson flowers, folded herself into the tight space, and waited. She slowed her breathing, smoothing it out, hoping Blanc wasn't blessed with superlative hearing—or were assassins chosen for their extraordinary senses? It seemed as though hours passed as she crouched there. Where was he? Had he seen her? Did he know that she was the one who triggered the alarm? Would the librarian have told him?

Perhaps he would give up, hoping to pick up her trail another day. She tried to stop her tumbling thoughts, to focus on the path, visible through her cloak of leaves and flowers. How long had it been—two minutes, ten? Her phone was in her pocket. Should she call Liz or Thomas? She couldn't call the police.

Blanc appeared, coming along the path from the direction she had been going. How did he get ahead of her?

He stopped at the top of the stairs, scanning across the park for long moments until a group of tourists, led by a perky guide waving her yellow umbrella, crowded the path behind him. He had to move or be engulfed by senior citizens. He swore at the leader and strode past her towards the exit.

Anne waited.

Chapter Fifteen

Earlier that day, Liz parked her car and boarded the sleek white and blue ferry waited at the dock in Hamilton, followed on by a man who left a scooter under a palm tree in one corner of the parking lot. His red and black helmet attached by a cable to his machine.

Liz wore a hat that afternoon, a white straw with a jaunty crimson rose pinned its crown, a green shirt and navy slacks. She carried a red and navy bag containing her purse, a sketchy lunch and a book with as much information as she would need about the nature reserves and their small ponds. She sat in a window, reading about the Gilbert Nature Reserve, her goal that day. She volunteered for the Bermuda National Trust, and was intent on becoming familiar with every nature preserve.

The Reserve comprised five acres, she read, and contained within it an old mansion that was Sandys Parish Community Centre. She wanted to follow the trails and see a stand of Bermuda cedar trees, once the main building material on the islands. Entrance was free, and the Reserve was quiet in the off-season, although she knew there would be a throng of schoolchildren on a field trip somewhere on the property.

She noticed that another visitor entered the park after she did, following along behind her on the meandering path. Ahead of her, she saw the entrance to a section of the Railway trail, through a tunnel of overhanging branches. A class of high school students filled the narrow walkway. Not for her. She turned aside and took a path that led directly to the stand of cedar trees, took out her camera and took several pictures. Bermuda cedar, otherwise Juniperus Bermudiana, once covered Bermuda and was thriving until the arrival of insect pests from the USA that killed ninety-nine percent of the trees. The resistant one percent were hoarded and encouraged until now stands of young trees were visible in every parish.

"Good morning, Doctor McPhail."

The man who had followed her along the path spoke from close behind.

"Good morning. I'm afraid you have me confused with my sister," said Liz, sweeping off her hat. The man in front of her, medium height, wore a ball cap and dark glasses. His skin was pale; his voice a pleasant baritone, accented, but Liz wasn't sure whether it was with German or some middle European language.

"I don't think so."

"What do you mean you don't think so? Who are you and what do you want with my sister?" Liz pulled off her sunglasses. She and Anne looked alike, but not enough that anyone who met one would mistake her for the other after a moment or two.

"So you are the sister. You must know where she is living."

Liz started to tremble. This was the man Anne was afraid of, the one she was sure murdered Nathan.

"I don't. She wanted to be alone for a while and left. That's what she's like," Liz lied. "She goes off with no explanation."

"I don't believe you." He pulled a gun from his pocket and showed it to her, returning it to his side pocket. "You play games with me, and you die."

"I wouldn't dream of playing games with you. I don't know where she is."

In the distance, Liz could hear the sounds of the school group she had passed. She knew that the cedar grove was always on the list for the younger kids, and maybe it was for the older ones too.

"I am sure you must know. We are going somewhere where you will tell me what you know."

"No, we aren't."

The teenagers burst from the woods, surrounding her and Blanc. The two teachers called to Liz.

"Liz, what are you doing here?" one woman said with a curious glance at Blanc.

"Researching for my volunteering. Can I join the class?"

"Of course."

Liz walked away from Blanc, feeling his eyes following her into the crowd of young people, most of them towering over her. She felt the muscles in her back contract, fearing a shot. She turned around when she reached the head of the group. She took a deep breath when she saw that he was gone.

Would he give up? Or would he be waiting for her at the ferry dock? Staying with the children might put them at risk. She needed to get back to Hamilton without going on the ferry and that meant a long taxi ride — or perhaps she could take the bus to the tip of the island and take the ferry to St. George's. Perhaps she should call the police, but would they believe her?

She followed the group of students as they walked back to Somerset Village. He would expect her to take the ferry or the bus to Hamilton. At least she thought he would. A bus was waiting at the stop, a number 12 going to the Dockyards. She could take it and then the ferry to St. George's.

A few minutes later she walked past a row of red British telephone booths, the kind the British no longer used, and up the wooden stairs to the ferry dock. The ferry, crowded with Japanese tourists from the cruise ship anchored in the harbor, seemed a haven, but her fingers turned white gripping the rail, as she watched the dock. The engine purred. The ferry groaned and moved away from the landing. She saw him then, getting off a motorbike and pulling off a helmet. She couldn't see his face. She knew she was conspicuous, with her white hat and fair hair. The ferry would get her to St. George's before he could make it there on the bike, but no one she could meet her there before he arrived. Dave was too far away in Hamilton, and Martin had a meeting all day at his job. She didn't know where Anne was. That man who came to see her, Quin something, his card was in her purse. Perhaps he would help her. Someone to tell anyway. She rummaged in her purse for the card and dialed.

"Yes." The neutral voice might have been the man who visited her.

"Is this Mr Randall?"

"Yes. Who is this?"

"Liz, Anne McPhail's sister. I need help, and I didn't know who to call."

"What is it?"

"That man that Anne saw at the gallery. I was in the Nature Reserve, and he showed me a gun, and he demanded that I tell him where Anne is."

"Did you?"

"No, no. A school group came, and I was able to get away. I'm on the ferry to St. George's but he saw me on board, and he has a bike. He'll be there soon after I arrive. Can you help me?"

"I'll be at the landing. Are there many on the boat?"

"No."

"Too bad. Try to come off with as many as you can." He hung up.

He would be there. The ferry entered the harbor, slipping by a cruise ship and anchored at the ferry dock. Liz couldn't pick Quin out of the crowd of people at dockside, but she trusted, needed to trust that he was there. When she stepped onto the dock, a man detached himself from a group lounging on a bench, mingled with the tourists for a moment and took Liz's elbow. In a moment she was rigid with fear.

"I'm Quin, Mrs Heath. Walk with me."

"Is he here?"

"I haven't seen him yet. I have a car parked in the lot, at the back. We have to be fast."

"Not a problem," Liz said, almost breaking into a trot to keep up with his long strides.

No shots came. Quin passed her into the car, and eased into the street, moving slowly as the tourists parted in front of him. He made the left turn out of the lot and into the maze of one-way streets. Liz watched for the helmet but didn't see it until they were past the airport on the causeway.

"There he is." Liz turned her head away, hoping Blanc hadn't seen her.

"Don't worry, Mrs Heath. I'm taking you to my office. From there we'll call the police."

"That woman won't believe me."

"We'll see."

Quin's office looked like any other cottage along the quiet street. Only a tree, a pine of some sort, in the yard and a scraggly poinsettia bravely growing along the pale green wall attempted to be a garden. Quin sat motionless in the car, waiting, then hurried Liz up the walk to the front door. He watched the street while he made two calls, one, Liz thought, to his boss, and the other to the police. He was connected to the chief and in a few words outlined Liz's story.

"You need to deal with your officer," Liz heard Quin say, and then, "I'll take her home."

"There'll be a cop on your doorstep. He'll speak to Spottiswood."

"Thank you, Quin."

Liz held out her hand to him, and he took it, giving it a careful shake before giving it back.

"I'll take you home."

Chapter Sixteen

Adrienne drummed on her steering wheel until security called up to the house and opened the gate. Her wheels scattered gravel when she accelerated up the hill to the front door. She flashed her id at a sputtering valet, refused him her keys and held her thumb on the doorbell.

"Identification, please?"

The man asking was tall and broad and American. She opened her wallet, snapping it shut when she thought he looked long enough.

"I called ahead to speak to Mr Wainwright and several of the maids here?"

"Mr Wainwright is not available at this time, but the maids are waiting for you, with Ms Wainwright and a lawyer."

"Why the lawyer?"

"Why are you here?"

She gave the man a second look. No weapon that she could see, but that only meant that the tailor who constructed his handsome suit was good at his job. Not your typical rent-a-cop or higher-end security. Perhaps he carried credentials of his own.

"Who are you?"

"John Malcolm. If you'll follow me..."

"Very well," she said and followed him through the reception hall to a door that led to a side wing of the house. The maids waited in a sitting room, bright with light from tall windows overlooking a garden, comfortable with casual upholstered furniture, and filled with the enticing scent of coffee.

"Inspector Spottiswood. I'm Candice Wainwright. Please sit down." Candice waved her into a plump chair across from two young women.

After she took their names, she asked Candice to leave her alone with them and their lawyer.

"I prefer to stay."

"I can't conduct a confidential interview with you present."

Candice looked at the lawyer who nodded his head, and she left.

At that she could have stayed, Adrienne thought. They knew nothing about anything that could have got Jasmine killed. She took them through the last days of Jasmine's life. It was all routine.

"There was one thing," the smaller of the two said. "Yes."

"She owed money to a man called Freddie, and she paid him off."

"How much?"

"A thousand."

"Where'd she get the money?"

"I don't know."

"When was this?"

"The day before she got killed."

The maids told her that Jasmine usually met her friends at a small cafe in Hamilton. Adrienne parked down the alleyway, walked up and in, letting the door slam behind her. The woman behind the counter tucked the pie she'd been cutting underneath a glass dome and spoke.

"Can I help you, officer?"

"Do you remember this girl?"

How did they always know she was police? She showed Jasmine's picture.

"Sure, Jasmine. She come in here with her friends every day. Sad day, sad day."

"Yes, it was. How was she the last time?"

"Bothered. They was talking about the murder in the art gallery, and Jasmine was lamenting 'bout wanting to get way from some man up at the Wainwright estate where she worked."

"Do you know who it was?"

"They called him the butler."

"Thanks," said Adrienne, getting up to leave.

"There was that other guy," the woman said before Adrienne reached the door. "I think he followed her."

"What other guy?"

"He come in here after the girls and sat where you did, eating cake and listening."

"What did he look like?"

"White. I don't mean he were a white man, though he was. I mean his hair was white, and his skin was dead white. His eyes were weird, grey and cold. You ever seen a shark? That's what he looked like—a white shark. And just as mean."

"Did someone pay you to tell me that?"

"Tell you what?"

"About the man."

"No. Ask Cal over there." She pointed to a man having a solitary meal in the corner.

"Cal, you remember that man what followed Jasmine the other day? Cal wanted to go after them, but I told him Jasmine could look after herself." At that, she started sobbing, and the interview was over.

The man confirmed what the owner told him. Now she knew that the man with the shark's eyes existed, and that Doctor McPhail's story true. Then why did she keep disappearing? Get her on your side, the American detective suggested. Probably too late for that.

Back at the office, her boss was waiting for her. "Deputy-inspector Spottiswood."

"Sir."

"Please sit down."

They were in her office, and he was sitting behind her desk. She sat on one of the hard wooden chairs she kept for visitors.

"Any progress in either of these murders?"

Adrienne reviewed the investigation from the finding of Nathan's body, to the latest information from the pair at the restaurant.

"So it appears that you've been chasing the wrong woman?"

"Yes, sir."

"You recall that after the last episode, I warned you against assuming that all Bermudians are innocent and all visitors, expats, whatever, are suspects."

"Yes, sir."

"Did you have any information that led you to believe that Doctor McPhail was other than a vacationer and a relative, I might add, of a prominent Bermudian family?"

"She was there; she was uncooperative; she tried to flee the jurisdiction."

"As to the last, you know that's absurd. I have questioned the officers who were present at the first investigation. They tell me you were antagonistic to Doctor McPhail from the outset, which might explain her reluctance to cooperate. Is she still your principal suspect?"

"No sir, she isn't, after today's interviews."

"I suggest you pay a call and talk to her again and listen this time."

He heaved himself out of her chair and strode from the room, leaving the door open behind him. Adrienne pushed it to and sat at her desk. He hadn't said it, but she knew she was on probation again. And the other officers at the scene who said she was antagonistic. Who were they? He also hadn't told her who called to complain. Somehow she didn't think Doctor McPhail possessed that kind of power, and for all the chief called her family "prominent", they weren't that important, at least not politically. Pay a call, he'd said. Very well, she would.

Anne would have welcomed a policewoman on her side as she exited the park onto Par-La-Ville Road, up to Church Street and past city hall to the bus station. How did he find her? She supposed that if he was staying at a downtown hotel, he might have seen her on the street by accident. Just luck. She could use a little of that. She climbed on the bus, said a general good afternoon and sat in a vacant seat behind the driver, where she could watch ahead as well as to the side. At the intersection, she saw a police car. The driver was Spottiswood. Again. Anne held her breath and turned away from the window. But the police car drove on. She got off at the stop closest to her sister's home, hurried up the street that backed on the property,

She slipped through the moon gate into the garden. Liz was likely at work, she thought. But when she opened the kitchen door she saw Liz and Thomas sitting at the pine table. A citrus perfume, lemon, cut for the tea they were drinking, filled the air. Anne let the door bang behind her.

"Anne. Did you come through the garden gate? I didn't hear a car," Liz said.

"I took the bus and walked up the back street. That man from the plane chased me in the park today."

She wrapped her shaking hands around a mug of tea, but put it down when the tea started to spill. Thomas reached over and took her hands in his.

"How did he find you?"

"I don't know, unless it was accidental."

"What were you doing in the park?"

"I'd been looking at newspaper records in the library. I saw him coming towards me and ran out the back door and hid in a shrub border."

Before they could ask any more questions, the doorbell rang. When Liz came back, Adrienne was with her.

"What are you doing here and why did you let her in without the lawyer?" Anne turned from Adrienne to her sister, not sure whom to be angry with.

"I've come to tell you that you are no longer a suspect in these murders," Adrienne began.

"Why not? What have you found out? And what do you mean, murders? Who else is dead?" Anne interrupted.

Adrienne took a breath and went on, "We found a young woman murdered, a maid who works at the Wainwright estate. When I investigated her movements, I discovered that a man closely matching the description you gave followed her. I've also been told by my superiors that there is no reason to go on investigating you."

"So you've been called off?"

"Yes, but I recognize that your behavior since you arrived has been that of a woman falsely accused. I thought I had good reason to suspect you, but now I don't, and I would like your help."

"You've put me through hell, left me alone to deal with a murderer and now you...you ask for my help?" Anne pushed the words out past the tightness in her throat that was cutting off her air.

"Yes, but...yes."

Anne stood with her back to the others, fighting to bring her emotions and her breathing under control. When she was calmer, she turned back and said, "How do you think I can help now?"

"Go over it all for me. Tell me what you know and what you think."

"Thomas, do you think I need the lawyer here?"

"Not if we record it, with Inspector Spottiswood repeating for the record her belief that you are no longer a suspect. If she won't do that, no deal."

"If you want a recording, we have to go to the station," Adrienne began.

"No." Three voices spoke at once.

"Very well, record it."

Thomas hit record on his phone. Adrienne formally repeated her statement that Anne was no longer a person of interest.

"Go ahead, Anne."

She went over the story again, from the moment on the plane when Blanc turned his fierce eyes her way to the last terrifying moments in the park. "

"Why do you think he's focused on you?"

"I don't know. I'm not the only person who knows about him. The CIA here must know and likely the top ranks of your service. Something is going on at the Wainwright estate, and I think he's going to try to kill someone or many someones, there. Maybe I pissed him off so badly that he wants to kill me. He passed up the opportunity; I don't know why."

"Too much heat," Thomas said. "If you died and the Wainwright girl, the conference would have been called off. His employers likely know that."

"He followed me today," Liz said.

"Where?"

"Out to the reserve." Liz sketched the story, including her rescue by a friend. She didn't mention Quin's name.

"I'm so sorry," Anne said.

"Not your fault."

"What's the conference about?"

Adrienne put her tiny black notebook on the table and wrote a heading on a fresh page. The stubby yellow pencil looked no shorter than when she interviewed Anne after the murder. Was she issued a new worn-down pencil every day, Anne wondered?

"I can't tell you."

The pencil skittered across the page.

"He took an oath," Anne said.

"Possibly your superiors would tell you if you need to know," he said.

"How can I find him, if I don't know what or who he's after?"

"If I were you," Thomas said, " I would proceed on the assumption that he's going to try to kill someone at the conference. As to whom, I don't know, and knowing the guest list won't help you. There are too many high- profile people, too many that have received death threats in the past and all of them with their security."

"What about this genealogy business? What does that have to do with the conference?"

"Nothing," Thomas said.

"Do you think this guy, Blanc, has any interest in the property rights?" Adrienne asked.

"I wouldn't think so. That's a separate issue," said Thomas.

"How will you find out if the land has changed hands illegally?" she asked Anne.

"I've gone as far as I can, with my feeble knowledge of Bermuda property law, but I'll give what I have to Margaret Smith, and if she wants to sue, I guess the courts will decide."

"Are you certain which property belonged to Noah Roberts?" Liz asked. "I seem to have heard something about ownership of the old factory being in dispute. Perhaps you should consider it as well as the Wainwright's."

"No, I'm not. I have to look at ordnance maps or land surveys."

"Dave has those at his office," Liz said.

"Will you take me there this afternoon?"

"Yes."

Moments later, the house was deserted: Anne and Liz going to Hamilton; Thomas to the Wainwright estate; and Adrienne back to her office.

   * * *

Thomas reached his hotel parking lot but didn't go in, but stood by his bike and waited.

"Was there something else, Adrienne?" he asked.

"Could we go inside and have a few words?"

"Yes."

They sat in the corner of the foyer, shielded from the curious desk clerk by a stand of potted palms.

"You seem to know what's going on at the Wainwright's house," she began. "Anne said, I think, that you "took an oath", and you suggested that I talk to my superiors. I prefer to talk to you."

"Anne meant what she said. I can't share anything with you."

"Can you tell me who John Malcolm is?"

"Malcolm? You mean Wainwright's butler or majordomo or whatever?"

"Do you know how long he's worked for them?"

"Few months. He replaced a man who died in a traffic accident in Florida."

"Do you know if he was checked out?"

"Everyone out there was. That's all I can say. Why?"

"I'm getting reports that he was harassing the maids out there. Maybe not the gentleman he pretends to be."

"I'll ask about him."

"I've been told there's CIA on Bermuda. Do you know anything about that?"

"Come on, Adrienne. If I did, I wouldn't tell you, and if I didn't, I couldn't tell you. Who told you?"

"That American cop, Anne's friend. He said I wasn't far enough up the food chain to know about it. If I'm far enough up to investigate the murders of these two Bermudians, I'm far enough up to be told what's going on." Adrienne started pacing.

"Sit down. That desk clerk's getting curious. I think you need to know, too. I'll see what I can do and get back to you."

"When?"

"Today."

Thomas watched her go, then walked down the steep hill to his villa. He reached into his jacket pocket for the key but left it there when he saw the door was ajar. He stood to the side to swing it open, then relaxed when he saw a familiar figure standing in front of the window.

"How've you been, Tom?"

"Good.

"You?"

"We have to talk about the situation," Quin said.

He shook Thomas's hand before sitting down in the one comfortable chair in the room.

"We do?"

"Your lady friend is causing too many questions to be asked."

"I don't think she chose to be kidnapped."

Thomas walked across to the minibar, pulled out a beer, held it up to Quin and reached for a second at his nod.

"She was poking around."

"That's what she does, especially when someone is accusing her of something she didn't do. You could have shut that down. Why didn't you or your boss make a call to the police here?"

Thomas shrugged off his jacket, hung it in the closet and sat down on the bed.

"We did, but they have their issues with a headstrong woman. That Spottiswood is hard to rein in."

He clinked his bottle against Thomas's and took a long swallow.

"What's the situation at Wainwright's?"

"Same old, same old. The Palestinians and the Israelis won't talk to one another until the SecState arrives on the weekend. They're all touchier than usual, especially the Israelis since it hit the fan in North Africa."

"Anybody out there stirring things up?"

"Someone is, but whoever is doing it is subtle, and no one has caught it yet."

"The cop, Spottiswood, was asking about Malcolm. She needs to know about our involvement on the island."

"Yeah? Maybe a thought. I'll see what I can find out about him. Telling her isn't our call. Her boss is the one to decide."

"He'll decide to tell her if we ask him to. If we don't, she's liable to cause trouble, blundering into our operation. As for Malcolm, I'll be out at Wainwright's tomorrow, perhaps with Anne. She might pick up something."

"You haven't told her what your job is?" Quin's voice held a warning.

"No, but I don't have to, she digs around anyway."

"That's dangerous, Tom. We don't want to tip our hand by dragging her out of harm's way. Maybe you should leave her behind. Tell her to spend the day at the beach."

"You don't know Anne."

"You need to keep her out of it."

"How about you look after your end of the job, and I'll look after mine, including Anne."

"Have it your way. I'm saying—"

Quin stood up, put his empty beer bottle on the dresser, and grabbed his jacket from the back of his chair.

"I'll see you tomorrow," he said.

Chapter Seventeen

The maps—modern and antique, real estate and ordnance —covered the tilt-top tables in Dave's drafting room. Anne brought out the legal description she'd found of Noah Roberts's property, and she and Dave pored over the maps to find the correct parcel of land. Half-an-hour later they found it, or so Dave thought. The land was, in fact, adjacent to the Wainwright property and didn't include any of it. What it did include, was the old warehouse or factory that Blanc used as a prison for his hostages.

"Poor Mrs Smith. That property's been in litigation as long as I can remember. Some American firm laid claim to it, a Bermudian company filed a counterclaim, and the case was before the courts for years. I'm not sure if it was ever resolved or who owns it now. I don't think there's any way she's going to get a piece of it."

"What's so special about it?"

"The land alone is worth millions. A long stretch of waterfront is rare on the market."

"The locks were new," Anne said."

She peered through a magnifying glass and traced the coastline from Wainwright's estate, past the warehouse to a headland jutting out to the sea.

"New?"

"Yes. New and shiny and silent. I think the one at the other end of the hallway into the building was new, too. Martin and Candice said they played there as children, and they didn't expect it to be locked."

"I didn't know the kids played in there. We did that too when I was a boy."

"When was it abandoned?"

"Just after the war. During the war, the Americans used it for something."

"What kind of something?"

Dave moved to the window overlooking the harbor. Anne remembered he'd done that when he was upset about her finding Nathan's body.

"Interrogation."

"How do you know?"

"My dad told me. It has the sea door; it's out of earshot of other buildings; it's not overlooked."

"Who were they interrogating?"

"German spies, but that's got nothing to do with now."

"It does if the Americans still have access. How did the guy Blanc know about it? For that matter, how did he find us in the middle of the Sargasso Sea? He has incredible resources. What's going on out there at Wainwright's?"

Dave turned back to her.

"I've no idea. The word around is that the Americans are there to pressure the Israelis and the Palestinians."

"What, again? That's worked so well in the past. Do you suppose the entrance is locked as well as the sea door?"

"You're not thinking of going out there?"

"Maybe there's more to find. That's where the briefcase was, and I stumbled over it."

"And what if Blanc is there? What if he's living there?"

"The man who came first class to Bermuda, wearing a thousand-dollar suit, is not living like a homeless guy," Anne said. "I'll think about it; maybe ask Spottiswood to take me out there."

"Ha. Don't do it, Anne."

"I'll see you later. Thanks for letting me look at your maps. Tell Liz that I'll be at your place about six."

She climbed into the taxi, settled back and asked the driver, "Do you know the old factory out by Tucker's Point. I don't remember the name of the street."

"Yes. There's not much out there."

"Just drop me as close as you can."

Anne closed her eyes and dozed off, waking with a start when the cabbie called her.

"We're here if that's what you want. I can't wait for you."

She paid him and took his number to call when she wanted to be picked up. It had been a factory or warehouse, Dave said, but looking at the modest facade of the two-story building, Anne thought it couldn't have been high-production. Somehow it didn't look like the kind of place to house spies and their interlocutors either. Too pink. She tried the handle of the front door. It didn't budge, but when she investigated around the side, she saw a door that stood slightly ajar.

The side door opened into a small anteroom. A derelict desk filled one side. Coat hooks beside the door that led into the larger space beyond suggested that it was the usual foot entrance to the building. A dustless path led from the outer to the inner door. Children, she supposed, although Martin hadn't told her how they usually got into the building. The inner door wasn't locked, and silent when she opened it. Odd, Anne thought. Children didn't come on their adventures with oil-cans.

The factory was used for the production of — what was it? — shoes and boots. That would mean rows of workers bent over old-fashioned sewing machines, the soft rhythmic sound of the pedals filling the air, or had the space held production equipment, noisy with the clatter of chain-driven lines, stamping out soles and uppers? But there were no pulleys, heavy ceiling hooks, deep indents in the floor, gashes or tears in the wooden floor, nothing to suggest heavy equipment had been torn from the room. The cavernous space swallowed the sounds of her footfalls and echoed them back to her. Light slanted from holes in the floor above.

Narrow stairs climbed to a partial mezzanine that came halfway up either side of the room. She looked into the rooms along it, found nothing and started back down the stairs.

When the taxi drove on without turning into the Wainwright estate, Blanc decided that the woman was going to the factory. Taking a back lane, he arrived before the taxi. He opened the side door, leaving it ajar. If she were curious enough to come inside, he would have her. From the mezzanine, he heard a car door slam and then sounds of the car leaving. Good, he thought. She'd sent away the witness. He slipped into an empty room.

He heard Anne's footsteps on the stairs and watched through a crack as she glanced into the room where he waited, hidden by the door. She started down the stairs.

All the frustration of the last week powered the hit he gave her back. She bounced off the stairs, screamed once, then fell silent when her head hit the floorboards. He'd reached the foot of the stairs, intending to make sure she was dead when he heard children's voices in the downstairs office. He started towards them. They're so young, he thought. Not much older than his kids. They wouldn't be able to describe him.

When he'd reached his room and left a message for Colette, he poured two inches of scotch into a tumbler and waited.

"What can I do for you?" she asked.

"I want you to check hospital admissions for that woman, McPhail, and the police reports of deaths."

"What have you done?"

"Just do what I ask."

"You are not sure she is dead. They are not going to be pleased with you."

"Do what I ask and spare me the comment. If there's nothing tonight, check tomorrow as well."

"Very well."

He sat on his balcony, looking out across the water towards the headland that contained Tucker's Point. Somewhere on the other side, the woman lay in the building, cold and broken and dying. He hoped she was dying, and that the children hadn't come into the room, or were too young to know what to do, or what they saw. Too much hoping. If she weren't dead, he'd have to kill her in the hospital. Colette said she was a pit bull, never letting go. And what about the children? He'd always drawn the line at killing kids. He wasn't sure that Colette would even agree to get him their names.

Marcus and Jeremy had played for weeks in the old factory, taking care to lock it up and hide the key each time they left. Brothers, Marcus was older, ten at his next birthday and Jeremy, seven. Their mother worked in the big house next door, and they were supposed to go home after school and were allowed to bike up the hill to meet her when her work day was over. That was what they were supposed to do.

They used to go in the sea door, but someone padlocked it. They found the key to the office door hidden under a rock next to a rusted-out bike stand near the entrance.

That day, however, they'd found the door standing open.

"I think we should go home," Jeremy said. "Someone might be here."

"Let's find out."

"Mom will be mad if they catch us."

"How could they catch us? We have our bikes and we can go on the trail."

They squeezed through the narrow opening left by the open door, passed through the hallway, stopped at the door into the factory floor, and peered through the dusty window.

"Someone's upstairs," Jeremy said. "We'll watch 'til they go."

"What if they come this way?"

"I told you we can go along the trail. Now be quiet, or they'll hear you."

They could see a woman walking down the stairs. But the woman wasn't alone. Behind her, he saw a man come out of a room further along the mezzanine and run down the stairs. He hit the woman with his shoulder, and she fell, bounced once off the stairs and hit the floor below. He was trying to kill her, Marcus thought. He pulled Jeremy to him and held his hand over the little boy's mouth, but too late. Jeremy screamed when the woman did. The man with the white hair saw them and started towards them. They ran, out the door and onto their bikes and up the trail towards the big house. They stopped when they reached the top of the hill and listened. Back towards the factory, they heard the roar of a motor-cycle engine, a big one.

"What will we do? I think she's dead." Jeremy was shaking and sobbing.

"We have to look at her."

"I don't want to. Maybe she's dead."

"We have to go back, Jeremy. You stay here if you want to."

Marcus left him in the tiny office and crossed to the woman on the floor. Her eyes were closed, and her mouth was bleeding a little, but he could see that she was breathing.

"She's not dead," he called. "Come over here."

"I'm scared."

"Me, too, but we have to get someone to help her."

"We'll get in trouble."

"We'll say we heard her scream and came to look. Come on. We'll get Mom."

Anne woke, stirred, and slipped into unconsciousness again. She didn't hear the boys and their mother arrive, nor the call to emergency services, nor the paramedics. Dust particles danced in the light that filtered through the grimy windows, and then faded from view as the sun dropped below the horizon. Adrienne stood beside the boys and their mother watching the paramedics work.

"What did you see," she asked.

"We saw the man with the white hair push the lady down the stairs," Jeremy blurted.

"I thought you heard her scream from outside?

"Marcus?" their mother asked.

"Don't be mad. We were in the office. The door was open, and we came in to see what was in here. We heard the lady walking upstairs and then she started to come down and then the man with the white hair came out and pushed her."

"Did he see you?"

"Yes, he looked at us, but then he ran away, and I heard his bike."

"Thank you, boys. I think you should take the boys home now, Mrs Cousins. I'll be in touch if I need anything more from them."

Adrienne settled back and waited for questions from her supervisor.

"So you think the children are in danger?"

"I don't know how he would get their names."

"He seems to have considerable resources. I assume you have a guard on Doctor McPhail's room."

"Yes. I'll visit the boys' mother and suggest she take them off island until we get him."

"Will that keep them secure or expose them in a jurisdiction where we can't protect them?"

"I'll have to give that some thought."

How could she know, with everything relevant being kept from her? She might as well ask. "Something is going on at the Wainwright estate, and I would like to know what it is. Are you able to tell me?"

"No," he said. He stood up, and the interview was over.

No, she thought. No. How was she supposed to get anywhere? Perhaps she would learn more at the hospital.

Chapter Eighteen

They stared at each other or the pale green walls. Liz sat in a dark green corner chair, hugging her chest, not speaking, barely able to breathe. Dave stood at the window with its view of the sea. Martin stretched his long legs into the middle of the room and rested them on a small oak table. Thomas walked in.

"I'm so sorry, Liz," he said, taking a seat beside her after shaking hands with Dave and Martin. "What happened?'"

"She was looking for evidence out at the old factory," Dave said. "I told her not to go, but you know how stubborn she is."

"Do they know why she fell?"

"No. Children found her, but as far as I know, they didn't see her fall," Dave said.

"How bad is she?"

"We don't know yet." Liz turned away as she started to cry again.

"What evidence?" Thomas asked Dave.

"She'd found that briefcase out there when they were kidnapped, and she thought she might find something more."

The door to the hallway opened again. This time it was a trim

Chinese woman, who asked, in a clipped British accent if they were Doctor McPhail's relatives.

"I'm her sister. My name is Liz Heath," Liz answered, "And this is my family and Anne's good friend, Thomas Beauchamp."

"Friend as a synonym for partner?" the doctor asked.

"Not precisely."

"Anne has a fractured ankle, which we have repaired with pins and a plate. She also has suffered a concussion, we think, although not a fractured skull. The CAT scan doesn't show any bleeding in or around the brain. She may have post-concussive symptoms for a few hours to weeks."

"This is her third concussion in the last two years," Thomas said.

"How severe were the other two?"

"One was a car accident. She wasn't badly hurt and went home from the hospital the next day. She didn't complain of a headache or anything afterwards. The second time she was hit on the head by a rifle butt and had a harder time recovering, but nothing that lasted more than a day or two."

"Was she otherwise injured in that assault?"

"No."

"As you may know, the effects of concussions can be cumulative. We'll have to keep her here until we're sure she can safely be discharged. She may not be able to travel by air for some time."

When she left, Liz spoke first. "She didn't tell me she'd been hurt before."

It almost hurt to speak, she thought. That must be what Anne felt when she choked up.

"Both times it was in Vermont. The first time she was forced off the road during a blizzard. The second time she was in the wrong place at the wrong time."

The door to the hallway opened again. This time it was Adrienne who walked in. Couldn't she leave them alone?

"I'm very sorry," she said, "but I have to ask you some questions."

"Why? Wasn't this an accidental fall?" Thomas asked.

"We have witnesses who saw her pushed down the stairs. Do you know where she'd been today?"

"She was at my office before she went out there," Dave said. "We found the actual land, the old shoe factory, that Mrs Smith contends or hopes is hers. Anne wanted to go out there to look for more evidence."

"More evidence?"

"She found a briefcase in the tunnel out there. Full of documents about the land and the inheritance, she said. She thought there might be something else."

"Why didn't you stop her?" Liz said.

"When can anyone stop her doing anything?" Dave said.

"Where did you go after I left you at the hotel?" Adrienne asked Thomas.

"Nowhere. I took a nap and woke up when Liz called me."

"I was at work," Martin said when Adrienne looked at him.

"I was shopping, and when I came back to Dave's office we went home," Liz said. "Why does it matter where we were? Do you think any of us would hurt Anne? I thought you realized that this man, Blanc, was the threat? What is the matter with you?"

"Adrienne, I need a word," Thomas said and walked her out the door and around to the elevators.

"Here?" she asked.

"Better in your vehicle."

Once inside her car, Thomas said, "Have your bosses said anything more to you about the event at the Wainwright estate?"

"Not a word."

"Okay, then you take me to your shop. I want to talk to your boss myself."

In reply, she turned the key, put the car in gear and drove away from the hospital.

Thomas sat across from Adrienne's boss and listened to all the reason's why she shouldn't be told about the CIA and the meeting on the Wainwright estate. She was impulsive; she chose to believe only Bermudians; she had no security clearance at all; she was on probation because of past errors.

"Why is she still on the case?"

"There didn't seem to be international involvement, and she is assigned to Serious Case."

"Token woman, is she?"

"If you must put it that way. We would have to answer a good many questions from women's groups and the newspapers if she were relieved of her post."

"She won't clear the cases unless she knows what's going on. At least to a certain level."

"Who would you have to consult before I told her?"

"No one."

The policeman looked across at Thomas whose credentials seemed to give him the authority to make this decision.

"On your head, then."

He buzzed his assistant and asked for Adrienne to be sent in. When she arrived, he walked out of the room, closing the door behind him.

"Adrienne, you'd better sit down," Thomas said.

"What is it?"

"I have to tell you that your two murders intersect with a major international meeting at the Wainwright estate. We believe the man you are looking for is also planning an assassination at the estate. We don't know who the target is."

"Who are "we"?"

"Organizations charged with making sure that nothing happens out there. When you were told there was an operating CIA unit on Bermuda, you didn't believe it or wouldn't believe it. International organizations require international security."

"The Bermuda Police Service can protect—"

"No, Adrienne. Don't even go there. Bermuda police don't have the resources or the experience. Stop wasting your time trying to implicate Anne or Adam or anyone else. We believe the murders are the work of a single man and his organization."

"If you know who he is, why haven't you stopped him?"

"He's a pro and he has an unusually well-funded group behind him."

"Who are you?" she demanded.

"That's something you don't need to know, but I've shown your boss my credentials."

"What do you want me to do?"

"I want you to protect Anne. He'll come after her again. We know that his flaw as an agent is that he makes it personal, and she's been in his way a few times now."

"You think he'll try at the hospital?"

"Likely. As soon as she can walk, I'll get her out of there."

"Who is he, the murderer?"

"He's called Blanc."

"Blank?"

"No, Blanc. French for white, because of his white hair and pale eyes."

"That's how the children from the factory described the man who pushed Anne. I'll look for him." She stood up and opened the door.

"Adrienne," Thomas called to her back. "You keep this to yourself. I mean from everyone who isn't me, even if you think whoever it is already knows."

"I will."

"You said the boys saw Blanc. Did he see them?"

"Yes, they thought so."

"They're in danger, too. What resources do you have to protect them?"

"I'll start by talking to their mother."

When she left, her boss came back in and sat across from Thomas.

"Well?"

"She might believe it. How long can you keep a guard at the hospital?"

"Not long. We're understaffed, and we have an outbreak of drug violence."

Thomas shook hands with him and left to take a cab back to the hospital.

Even the soft tick of the cardiac monitor hurt. Anne moved her eyes to look at the clock on the wall of the nurses' station. That motion started a wave of nausea and dizziness. When it settled, she opened her eyes. 8:15 the clock read, but was that morning or night. The lighting was low; the nurses murmured at the desk. Not enough bustle for eight in the morning, she decided. So it was night and she was in the ICU. She was thirsty, in spite of the intravenous in her left arm. Where was her nurse? She tried an exploratory groan, moved her arm and watched her heart rate on the monitor jump.

A young black woman— Bermudian by her accent— hustled into the room and asked Anne how she was feeling.

"Headache, thirsty, stupid."

Her tongue stuck to the roof of her mouth, making the word emerge as "thupid."

"Stupid? Do you mean stunned?"

The nurse held a straw to her lips. Tepid water, Anne thought. Who knew it could be as refreshing as a beer on a hot day?

"No, foolish. Walking into an abandoned building by myself. What happened to me?"

"You fell on the stairs," she answered.

She copied the messages that flashed on the monitor above Anne's head onto her clipboard.

"Why?"

"Why did you fall?"

"Yes."

"I have no idea."

The nurse checked the monitors again, asked Anne if she needed anything for pain and gave her another sip of water. Anne took an inventory of her body, starting with her toes. Her right leg fell back with a thud when she managed to lift it a few centimeters.

"What's wrong with my right leg?"

"You have a broken fibula and a torn tendon. Doctor Neve took you to the operating room and repaired them."

Fibula, Anne thought. Not too bad. She might be in a walking cast. It must have been bad to need repair. Sometimes, they were left to heal.

"And my head?"

"Concussion, no fracture."

"Another one. Damn," she said and drifted off to sleep.

A sudden jolt and a stab of pain woke her. She was being moved from a stretcher to a bed.

"Sorry, Anne," a cheerful voice apologized. "All done."

She was fussed over, tucked in, a call button pinned to her pillow, and told to go back to sleep. She lay, wide-awake, staring into the darkness and wondering what she was going to do now. She turned on the light and threw the sheet off her leg. A cast, split in two to allow for swelling, enveloped her leg from toes to knees. She should be able to walk with crutches in a day or so, but how was she going to get back home? The stairs to the plane would be a challenge. Tomorrow's problem, she thought and closed her eyes.

A knock awakened her. Thomas and Liz stood at the end of her bed. Why was Liz crying about a broken leg? That wasn't like her.

"Don't cry, Liz. They fixed everything, and I'll good as new in a few weeks."

"Someone tried to kill you, Anne," Thomas said, taking her hand. Liz brought a chair close to the other side of her bed and sat down.

"I was pushed?" How did he get there ahead of her? How did he always know where she was going?

"Yes," Thomas answered.

"Why didn't he make sure I was dead?"

"There were children there."

"Children. Can you find out who they were so I could thank them? They must have been so frightened but they helped me anyway. It must have been Blanc. How did he know I was there?"

Question followed question until finally, Thomas said, "He likely followed you from Dave's office."

"He'll try again."

"You're out of the way now. Why would he?" Liz asked.

"Personal. I think he's made it personal now."

"Spottiswood put a guard on the room," Thomas told her.

The nurse came into the room, hurried Liz and Thomas out, and did her eleven o'clock vitals. Anne turned out the light, but sleep wouldn't come for many hours, and when she slept, a nightmare vision of Blanc— white hair and evil eyes and sharp teeth — haunted her dreams.

Chapter Nineteen

Adrienne sat in her office, drawing outlines of the two cases, looking up from time to time to see her boss, in his glass-enclosed, corner office looking at her. How long would he keep her on if she couldn't solve these murders? She closed her computer, unlocked her file drawer, took out her purse and put the computer inside. She glanced again at her boss. Damn it all, he knew the press was outside, and he was leaving her to deal with it. It would have to be no comment to everyone, even Paula.

A gaggle of the press gathered outside the police building, Paula among them. She followed Adrienne to her car, trailing behind her several others, including a reporter for a New York paper.

"Inspector, what can you tell us about the accident at the old factory? Has the Canadian doctor died?" Paula began.

"Have you arrested the Canadian for the murders?" called the American reporter.

Several more press ran towards them, shoving microphones and cameras in Adrienne's face, shouting questions, pushing each other to get closer and that perfect shot, or quote.

The reporter held her car door in a death grip. "Who were the children?"

"None of those details is being released at present," Adrienne answered. She closed her car door, cutting off the questions, but fortunately not the reporter's hands.

"Later," Paula mouthed at her through the windshield.

The New York reporter climbed on his rented motorbike and followed Adrienne out of the parking lot.

Minutes later Adrienne stopped in front of a tiny house set back from the street. A stacked stone wall restrained a patch of grass and a solitary shrub. A cracked walk led up to a broad but short set of stairs to the blue front door. Weeds sprouted in the cracks of the walkway, little ones, speaking to the neglect of a day or two by its frightened owner, but the steps and the stoop were well-swept, and the window in the door sparkled. Mrs Cousins, a petite black woman with a decided Jamaican accent, answered the door.

"May I come in," Adrienne said, showing her warrant card.

"Of course. I do remember you, Deputy Inspector."

She led the way into a minute front room—a comfortable, casual space with mostly wooden furniture, softened with pillows in orange and vibrant green. Adrienne removed the cushion from a straight-backed chair and sat.

"I'll take that for you," Mrs Cousins said and sat down opposite her. "What have you come to tell me?

"We have some concerns that your boys may be in danger from this man who pushed Doctor McPhail. I need to go over it all again. You remember that the first story was that they heard her scream, and the second was that they watched from the office. Could I ask the boys some more questions?"

"What kind of danger? What are you going to do? What can I do?" She held the pillow on her lap in a white-knuckled grip, and her voice shook.

"Let me talk to the boys. Are they frightened?"

"Now that it's all over, they're very excited. They have no idea that they're in danger themselves."

She left the room, returning with the boys, sitting them down and telling them to answer truthfully.

"Marcus," Adrienne said to the older boy, whose pale cocoa-colored face was punctuated by frightened blue-green eyes. "I want to ask you again what you saw at the factory. First of all, were you there before?"

"Yes," he answered with a sideways glance at his mother, who gripped her pillow tighter but said nothing.

"How did you get in?"

"There's a key under a rock. A man comes on Tuesdays and looks inside, and we saw him put it there."

"Do you know who the man is?"

"No."

"Is that how you got in today?"

"No, the door was open a little. We thought someone might have left it that way by accident or that there was someone inside, so we squeezed through. We looked into the factory through the window in the inside door."

"What did you see?"

"The lady what got shoved was starting down the stairs. The man ran out of one of the rooms upstairs and hit her in her back with his shoulder before she could hold onto the bannister. She was screaming but then her head hit the floor and she stopped. We thought she was dead, and that he would kill us too when Jeremy screamed, but he looked at us and ran out the door. I heard his motorcycle, a big one, drive away."

"How do you know it was a big one?"

"I heard the engine," said Marcus, his tone questioning her ability if she didn't know something so simple.

"What did he look like?"

"I already told the other policeman."

"I know, but I want to hear too. Maybe you remember some more details. Kids your age are good at remembering," she coaxed.

"He was tall as Uncle James."

"About six feet," his mother interjected.

"And he wasn't fat or skinny," Jeremy piped in. He was hiding, huddled behind his brother, peeping out at her, but there was more curiosity than fear in his almond-shaped hazel eyes. He was darker than his brother and thinner.

"His hair was white, and he was real white, whiter than most white guys. He looked real mean."

"Do you think he got a good look at you?"

"Yes," both boys said.

"Mrs Cousins, I think you should take the boys away for a while. Is there anywhere you can go, off Bermuda?"

"I could stay with my brother in Jamaica, but I can't afford the flight."

"We have to protect them, so I think the department would pay. We think that man who attacked Doctor McPhail has killed two other people, and the boys can identify him."

"I don't believe this is happening to us." The mother cried, rocking back and forth on her chair. The boys went to her, patting her shoulder, the younger one crying as well.

"It will be over when we get him, Mrs Cousins."

"I don't believe it. Even if you get him, he'll get off. Nothing ever happens to anyone here. We'll have to run away and hide, and we'll never be safe."

Her voice rose in a wail, easily heard by the American reporter sitting outside the house. He asked a passerby who lived in the house where the woman was crying and was told Mrs. Cousins and her sons Marcus and Jeremy. He left for his hotel, and within a few minutes, the boys' identity was on the paper's website.

Adrienne returned to her office and was met by her angry boss.

"Those bastard Yanks have spread the boys' names all over the web."

"We have to get them off the island."

"Get them and bring them here."

Adrienne drove as fast as she dared on the twisting streets

through the back lanes to where the boys lived. Within minutes she hustled the family into her vehicle and drove back to the station.

"Mrs Cousins, this is Chief Inspector Dowland."

"I'm very sorry for your trouble," the big man said, enveloping her tiny hand in his massive ones. "We would like to get you off-island for a while. I understand you have relatives in Jamaica where you could stay?"

"I have my brother James. He would take care of us."

"We can have you on a flight in two hours. Would you like to call your brother from here?"

"I can use my cell phone."

"That isn't safe anymore. We'll have to get you a new one."

"What about my job?"

"Deputy-Inspector Spottiswood will visit your workplace and inform him. Where do you work?"

"At the Wainwright estate. I'm his daughter's personal maid."

"We'll look after it."

Two hours later the family was on a flight to Jamaica, accompanied by a police constable.

Across the island, Blanc turned on his laptop and googled — Bermuda, murder, children. Buried on the second page of results he found the website for the tabloid the American reporter worked for and the information about the boys. Good, he thought. He wouldn't have to talk to Colette and listen to all the reasons why he should leave the boys alone.

But where were they? Perhaps he would need her after all? He tried the local papers but found nothing. What would the police do? Get them off the island, he supposed. He would have to call Colette.

"What can I do for you?"

The precise Swiss-French accent began to irritate him. She didn't want to be helpful; she wanted to control him or get rid of him. He could imagine her calling the controller every time he asked for information.

"I want you to look at the passenger lists from Bermuda over the last day, looking for a woman and two boys."

"Do you have names?"

"The boys are called Jeremy and Marcus Cousins. I don't know their mother's name."

"They will not be happy if you kill children."

"Just get me the lists. I'm not killing anyone, but I have to be sure they've left the island before I can go in with my work," he lied.

"I have found only one family such as you describe, travelling to Jamaica. Their destination address is not available, and they are travelling with an escort, likely police."

"Good, so they're off the island."

"Yes.

Blanc exited the airport and took a cab to the Pegasus Hotel in Kingston. Once in his room, he called Colette. "I need to know where the children and their mother

are staying."

"Where are you?"

"Get me the information."

"I'll have to ask permission. This has gone too far."

"Get me that information, Colette. Don't get in my way."

Even in her far-off office, an ocean away, protected by her company's security, Colette knew a moment of fear. She knew his reputation, especially with women. Her fingers had been working, and she gave him the information he wanted. A phone number for the home came up in the database she was searching, but she didn't give him that. Her elegant fingers tapped the table for a few moments, then called a number in Bermuda. A few sentences and she made another call, this one to Jamaica.

≈

Blanc got into the front seat of a taxi in front of the hotel and gave the driver the address.

"No way, man. I don't go down there, not ever."

"You do today," he said, giving him an American hundred-dollar bill.

"I can get you close, but that's all. I ain't waiting."

Blanc handed him another hundred.

"That buys you five minutes, man. That's all."

"That's all I need."

They drove through a shantytown of tin-roofed shacks and desolate, abandoned buildings, their windows replaced with battered plywood covered with colorful graffiti. From time to time Blanc could see small groups of men, cigarettes hanging from careless lips below cautious eyes that followed their progress deeper into the ghetto.

"Do you know where you're going?"

"Not anymore. We have to ask."

"Ask."

They stopped beside a woman trudging through the dust, two small children clinging to her multicolored skirt and a baby in a sling across her chest.

"Do you know where this is?" the cabbie asked, showing her the address.

"Turn left at the corner to the pink house with the porch. Do you know whose house that is?"

"No."

She mentioned the name of one of the feared leaders of a street gang, and then turned and hurried away from them, back the way she'd come.

"Man, we shouldn't go there. That house's gonna be guarded good, and they don't ask, they shoot."

"Drop me at the corner and wait."

"You too white to walk these streets."

"My problem. Wait five minutes."

Blanc got out of the car, used its bulk to shield his body and sheltered behind a building on the corner. A few houses down he saw more young men, some slouched on the porch of the pink house, watching the street, some standing beside a black SUV. All of them were armed. A woman and two boys were hustled out the front door. The family and two men climbed into the waiting vehicle and sped away.

Blanc pounded the wall with his fists and then ran back to the cab.

"Follow them."

"No. You might as well kill me, man, cause I ain't gonna do that."

Blanc leaned into his seat. The cabbie was right, he thought. No way could they follow through that maze of streets, and he couldn't fight his way into wherever they were going.

"Go back to the hotel."

Why did they change houses at that moment? Did they know he was coming? The only one who knew was Colette. Colette. She was always questioning his requests, warning him, obstructing him. Never again. He would deal with her when he finished in Bermuda.

"Who was that guy the woman said lived in the house?"

"He the boss of the gang that owns this neighborhood."

Blanc watched the street for signs of the vehicle that held his targets but he only saw the men slumped in front of the buildings, armed, he now recognized, with automatic weapons, all with the same type, the rifle produced by the company he worked for. Colette could have found the number; he was sure she called to warn them. That was the last time she got in his way.

The boys huddled together in the corner of the big black car. Their mother sat beside them, twisting her scarf in her hands, silent tears dripping down her face.

"Where are we going?" she asked. "My house."

"I thought that was your house."

"No. You didn't think I lived down there? I have a house in the hills."

"If he found us in one he can find us in this one too."

"No one but me and Raymondo know about this one," he said, clapping the driver on the shoulder.

The route took them away from the city and up into the hills. The air cleared, perfumed by breezes from the mountain. The streets became broad and smooth, bordered by vast lawns and mansions, some hidden, all but their roofs obscured behind locked gates. They turned into the driveway before one of the gates. The driver inserted a key into a security pad and punched the numbers. The gate swung smoothly inward, and as quietly closed behind them.

A two-story, pale blue mansion perched on an elevated lawn, a carport at the side sheltering two vehicles, an elegant black Cadillac and an ominous green Hummer.

"This is your home, James?"

"Yes, mine and Alicia's. You remember Alicia?"

"Yes."

She remembered Alicia, a sixteen-year-old girl when she last saw her. Now she possessed all this.

Later, after tea, watching the boys sliding joyously into the pool, she asked how long they could stay.

"As long as it takes those fool cops to find the white man," her brother answered.

"And if they don't."

"Then we will. He's gone back to Bermuda."

"You know this for sure."

"Yes."

Mrs. Cousins drew a breath, sank back into her deck chair and closed her eyes. She left Jamaica to run from the drugs and the violence, and here she was, living in a home paid for by crime, watching her boys play. If she stayed very long, she knew they would be drawn into that world. But she could feel the seduction. All that Bermuda held for her was the job of tending to Ms Wainwright's needs, mostly her clothes and picking up after her. Here, she would be looked after. Perhaps if she sent her boys to the same school that James's sons attended, they would escape the criminal life. James broke into her thoughts.

"You don't have to go back. I'll buy you a house, set up a fund for you, clean money, so you can live without picking up after a lazy girl."

"Thank you, James. I'll think about it for a little."

But she knew that she'd had enough. She couldn't go back to face twenty more years of the same drudgery, with a skimpy pension at the end and no guarantee the boys would stay out of harm there. She could see James leaning back, a satisfied smile on his face. He knew it too.

Chapter Twenty

The nurse tuned on the light, and bustled around the bed, taking the blood pressure cuff from her trolley and fitting it to Anne's arm, then sticking a temperature probe in her ear. The beep elicited a satisfied grunt from the nurse and the blood pressure a question.

"Do you feel at all faint, Anne?"

"No. My blood pressure is usually low—one hundred and five over sixty, something like that."

"We'll get you up slowly, shall we?"

"I'm dry. Someone took the iv out last evening."

"Haven't you been drinking?"

"No, sleeping."

"How is your headache?"

"Not too bad, considering."

Hospital routine filled the rest of the morning: doctors' visits, one an orthopedic surgeon and another, a neurosurgeon; a physiotherapist to get her up and walking with crutches; another doctor who would take overall care. Liz arrived to visit her late in the morning.

"Hi. I thought I would find you looking better but you look awful— pale and sweaty and those sunken eyes."

"Nice to see you too, Liz."

"I'm sorry."

"The morning was busy. But check the corner."

Liz looked across at a pair of shiny aluminum crutches leaning against the wall.

"Are you up already?"

"Yes, I only broke my fibula. The tendon is the main problem, that and the concussion. They would have sent me home except for that. The concussion is the worst."

"There's a guard outside your door."

"Is that to keep me in or Blanc out?"

Liz laughed and said, "Blanc out. Adrienne doesn't think you're a murderer anymore, but she's afraid he'll try to kill you here."

"I am too."

Later, Adam and Erin came in, wrapped in the delight of newly-engaged couples. Anne admired the ring and heard about their plans to live in Erin's loft until they decided about law school for Adam.

"When is your flight?"

"This afternoon. Do you think you'll be able to visit Culver's Mills this year?" Erin asked.

"Not likely before Christmas. I want to go to Europe when my leg heals and if the concussions aren't giving me too much trouble."

"Have they found the guy who did this to you?" Erin asked.

"I don't think they can. I didn't see anyone, but perhaps the children did."

"Won't they be in danger, too? "I hope the police think of that."

And then Anne was alone, the blinds closed against the afternoon sun, and the pain in her head worse in the quiet of her single room. She wished the guard would come in and talk to her. She wished Thomas would come and explain what was going on. And then she wished the nurse would come and give her something for her headache. She slept, for only a few minutes she thought, but when the aide with the dinner tray rattled into the room and flicked on a light, she saw that the sun had gone and she knew that she'd slept for hours.

* * *

Thomas sat by her bed, waiting for her to waken. What the hell was he going to tell her? She was in no shape to hear about the meeting or his role in it.

"Don't trouble her," the doctor said. "The concussive symptoms will get worse if she's under stress, or even forced to think deeply about something."

"Thomas?" Anne said.

"I'm here, dear heart."

"What happened to me?"

He told her again about the old factory and the fall and the concussion and the fracture.

"The children?"

"Safe. They've been sent off-island with their mother. You're supposed to rest, not think, just be."

"I'll try," she said and drifted off again. The nurse came in, and Thomas left.

Outside the hospital, he called Quin and arranged to meet for dinner.

Quin sat at a table at the far end of the terrace, no one near him and a full sight line to the entire space. Not that there was much to see, Thomas thought. It was early for dinner, and most of the tables stood empty. Thomas took a seat with his back against the railing, where he too, could watch the terrace.

"What's happened to Anne?" Quin asked.

"Blanc attacked her in that old factory, pushed her down the stairs. Broken leg, concussion. Two little kids were there, and Blanc took off without finishing her."

"He'll try again. Her and the kids."

"They have a cop outside her door, and the kids are in Jamaica."

"What about Saturday?"

"We'll have to see how she comes along. I don't like it." Thomas stopped talking as the server came up.

After they ordered dinner and a beer each, Thomas said again, "I don't like it."

"She knows what he looks like."

"By now he's changed his appearance."

"Doesn't she know him by his walk?"

"Yes."

"Then?"

"She's been accused of murder, kidnapped, assaulted, and you want to put her in harm's way again?"

"We need what she knows."

"We'll have to talk to her together, later, when she's better."

"We don't have much time, Tom."

Chapter Twenty-One

Blanc opened the case of contact lenses and fitted them onto his eyes, changing first one, then the other from its cold grey-white to a warm brown. His hair was now a dull auburn, hidden under a blue baseball cap dedicated to the Yankees. He dressed in a green, long-sleeved shirt and dark blue jeans, scuffed runners and slung a messenger bag over his left shoulder. He tucked his gun into the waistband of his jeans, under the tail of his shirt.

He asked at the desk for the directions to the surgical floor and was told there were two, Curtis and Cooper. He guessed Curtis and took the elevator to the ward.

There was no guard outside any of the rooms on Curtis, but on Cooper, he saw a bored young policeman propped against the wall opposite a room at the end of the corridor. He watched the policeman from an empty room. Sooner or later he would have to leave, judging from the coffee cups stacked in the trash basket beside him.

A few minutes later the guard spoke into his shoulder radio, raced past the room Blanc was hiding in and paused at the nursing station long enough to call out to them that he was leaving. Blanc

walked out into an empty corridor, towards the room at the end
that was Anne's.

At the other end of the corridor, Anne stepped out of the elevator, negotiated the track of the door in spite of her crutches and
turned towards her room. A man with nut-brown hair walked
towards the end of the corridor and her room. No sign of her guard.

That was him, she thought. That was his walk. That was Blanc.
That stupid guard insisting his job was to stay at the room door
instead of with her. Her throat tightened, and she fought against
the panic. Where could she hide? She swiveled, lost her balance,
steadied herself against the wall and then propelled herself in the
opposite direction, away from the killer and into an adjoining ward.
No one sat at the nursing station or in the lounge beyond it, and
they would be dead-end traps anyway. No way out. Further along,
she heard the urgency in the voices coming from a treatment room.
A child was in trouble. That would keep the nurses occupied.
Perhaps he would give up? Had he seen her at the elevator?

Would he search for her on this ward?

A baby wailed in the next room, that half-moaning, half-crying
sound of an exhausted infant too tired to sleep. A cart outside the
door holding gowns and caps and gloves told her that the infant was
in isolation. She grabbed one of each and went through the sterile
area into the room beyond. The indirect light behind a valance cast
a dim glow on the room. She stood with her back to the door,
waiting for her eyes to adjust.

The baby stopped crying for a moment and watched her
through the bars of the crib. Anne pushed a rocking chair closer to
the crib. Abandoning her crutches, she balanced on her strong leg
and lightly on her cast, put on a gown and cap and mask and groped
for the side release on the crib. When she felt secure, she picked
him up, felt for the chair behind her knees and sat back holding him
against her chest. He smelled of his bath and oil and that other
sweet smell of all well-cared-for infants.

She slid her crutches under the crib and hoped he didn't see them in the room as he walked by. The baby, soothed by the rocking, fell asleep on her shoulder. Anne sang a soft lullaby and watched the reflection of the hallway in the mirror over the sink.

A man's face appeared, peering into the room. His hair was brown or red, but she couldn't see his eyes, couldn't tell if it was Blanc or someone checking on the baby. She continued to rock, and at last, he moved on. After what seemed to be an hour, he passed by going in the opposite direction. Anne tucked the baby back into his crib and caressed his tiny head until he settled back into a deep sleep. She rescued her crutches from underneath the crib and opened the door a crack.

Two nurses stood talking to Blanc. They shook their heads and pointed towards the elevators. A remote voice overhead announced the visiting hours were over. A third nurse joined the group and escorted Blanc to the elevator bank. When the doors closed behind him, Anne crutched back to her room, hauled her sweatpants on over the cast, scrabbled in her suitcase for a jacket then took the elevator to the main floor. She couldn't see anyone that looked like Blanc in the lobby. She had a little money in her purse and her cell phone, but where could she go?

She pushed the automatic opener for the heavy front door and struggled through. The driver of a taxi standing at the curb jumped out and held open the back door of his cab.

"Where would you like to go?" he asked, then said, "Are you all right, lady? Maybe I should help you go back inside?"

"I still have pain in my leg," she said, "but the doctors say there'll be no problem."

"Until you have to go back and get it broke and set again."

"You had some trouble with the orthopedics here?"

"You could say so, you could say so."

"I hope I have more luck."

She gave him the name of Thomas's hotel and leaned back into the seat. Her reflection in the driver's mirror told her why he wanted to take her back in. Pallor outlined the dark circles under her eyes.

Blanc knew about her sister and Mrs Smith and likely the little apartment, but maybe not. He might know about Thomas, and she didn't want to lead him there. She told the driver she changed her mind and gave him the address of the apartment.

When the door closed behind her, she dropped onto the sofa, lifted her casted leg onto an ottoman, and tried to think about what to do next. Pain in her leg reminded her that she had no painkillers and no way to get any. She heaved herself out of the chair and took three steps across the room to a side door leading to a patch of grass, two green plastic garden chairs, and a glass-topped table. She sat down, put on her dark glasses and turned her face to the sun. The soft sweet fragrance of the oleander hedge eased her into sleep.

She drifted awake, to the sound of children's voices piping through the hedge.

"I think she's sleeping," a little girl said.

"I think we should tell her about the man. Mommy said so."

What man, Anne thought, stirring. What man were they talking about?

"Lady, hey lady."

Anne opened her eyes to see two small faces peering through the hedge.

"Yes," she answered.

"What's wrong with your leg?"

"Broken. I fell," she expanded, knowing the next question would be "how?"

"Why did the man come and ask Mommy about you?" asked the little girl.

"What man?"

"The man with the white hair."

The knot that had been in Anne's stomach all day twisted.

"What did your mom say?"

"She said you went away."

Good, but he knew where she'd been living, and he would be back.

Anne struggled to her feet, waved good-bye to the children and went into the house. When the door closed behind her, she fought off tears and called another cab. She would have to go to Thomas's hotel. There was nowhere else, and she needed help.

The cab stopped at the hotel entrance. Anne knew she couldn't make the walk down to Thomas's villa. Her leg throbbed and her shoulders ached from the burden of moving her from place to place. She staggered as a wave of dizziness and nausea hit her. This concussion was going to be harder to get over than the last. She huddled in a wide wicker chair, hidden, she hoped, behind the screen of an ancient Mandeville vine, and rested her leg on the edge of its green porcelain pot.

From where she sat she could see the lobby and driveway beyond. She called Thomas, only to hear the ring click over to message.

"Thomas, I left the hospital because Blanc was there searching for me. I'm at your hotel."

When she hung up, she remembered that she hadn't said she was in the lobby.

He stood the bike close to the gate. He didn't need to peer again at the paper he took from Jasmine. The code was simple. If it worked tonight, it would be no problem on Saturday to slip onto the estate early.

He tapped in the numbers and waited. Nothing. No slow movement of the high iron gates. He pounded the pillar in fury then ran for the bike.

Why did they change it again? Jasmine. Why did anyone care if the maid was killed? She wasn't the one trusted with the code. He called Colette when he reached his hotel.

"The code has been changed."

"All this killing is drawing attention to the operation.

"You must be more careful."

"Don't tell me what to do."

"Have you another plan?"

"My operation, my plan. Someone is tipping them off. Was it you? They were ahead of me in Jamaica, too. That was you, too."

"The controller will want to know what you intend."

"Don't get in my way, Colette."

"What shall I tell him?"

"Fuck off."

Chapter Twenty-Two

Anne hid behind the palms, soothed by the spatter of rain on the cobblestones in the driveway until the nosy woman at the desk started whispering to the concierge and sending glances her way. Thomas still hadn't called back. Adrienne. She could go to her or call her, and she would come. She called, but the man at her office said that Adrienne was out. It would have to be a cab again. She hobbled to the edge of the driveway and asked the doorman to get her a taxi. She asked for the police station, put her head back against the seat and closed her eyes.

"Who that damn fool?"

The driver hit the brakes hard. Anne sat up with a jolt of pain in her head, wondering for a moment where she was and who was shouting at her.

"What's happened?"

"See that bike back there— the guy in the red and black helmet — he cut me off."

Anne knew there must be many red and black helmets on the island, but she only knew the one that might be coming to Thomas's hotel. She swiveled every few seconds to make sure the motorcycle hadn't turned around to follow them. And where was Thomas? Why hadn't he answered her call?

"Please hurry," she said.

Anne struggled up few steps, slippery from the recent rain, to the front door of the police building. She pushed on the cumbersome front door, gave up and used the handicap button, tripped crossing the sill, and fell to one knee, screaming as the pain from her leg rocketed up to her hip. A nearby policeman helped her to her feet and supported her to a chair.

"Who are you?" he asked.

"My name's Anne McPhail, Doctor McPhail. I called earlier. I must see Deputy-Inspector Spottiswood."

"She's out."

"I'll sit here quietly and wait, shall I?" Anne said.

She heard the sound of sand rushing through her head, saw the light fade, and then nothing.

"Anne, Anne, wake up."

People here were always yelling at her. Why was this annoying woman yelling? Didn't she know her head hurt? She opened her eyes to Adrienne's anxious face.

"Did I faint?" Anne asked.

"Yes."

"I'm sorry. It's the pain, you see," she said and closed her eyes again.

"She's gone again, Inspector. Shouldn't you take her to the hospital?"

"She ran from the hospital to come her. Something's happened. If she stays awake long enough, she'll tell us."

"I haven't fainted. I'm awake now."

Anne felt the rough fabric of the couch that supported her; smelled stale coffee and sweat; closed her eyes against the light of an overhanging lamp: the staff room.

"He searched for me at the hospital and at the apartment where I stayed."

She told Adrienne what she saw and what the children told her.

"You think he's changed his appearance?"

"Yes. His hair is a dull red-brown, like a squirrel in the fall. I didn't see his eyes. The only thing he can't disguise is that little hesitation when he walks. I watched him at the hospital. He looked in every room on Pediatrics until the nurses told him to leave. What am I going to do, Adrienne? He knows where my family is and maybe Thomas. Where can I hide?"

"What happened to the guard at the hospital?"

"I went to physio, and when I came back, he was running out. He yelled to the nurses that he had to go. I don't know why."

"Find out," Adrienne snarled at someone nearby.

"Thomas isn't answering his phone, and he hasn't called me today. I'm afraid something has happened to him."

"Perhaps he's out at Wainwright's? I'll find out."

When she came back, she said, "He's in his room at the hotel. Do you want to go there or back to the hospital? I can put a guard on you there."

"I'll go to the hotel."

"I'd rather you go back to the hospital, or let me put you in protective custody here."

"No, I want to find Thomas."

"If you insist."

"I do."

The police constable who accompanied her back to the hotel commandeered one of the scarlet-topped golf carts used by the staff to move about the grounds. She let Anne off at the villa.

"Do you want me to stay, Doctor McPhail?"

"For a moment."

She opened the door with her key. Thomas and another man sat on the patio.

"Anne. Why aren't you in the hospital? What's happened?"

Anne waved to the constable, watched her drive off, and closed the door. She crossed the room to the terrace doors, passed Thomas and stepped outside.

"Anne, Quin. Do you want something to drink?"

"Some white wine, please."

When he brought back the wine, he kissed her and sat down.

"Quin, I think you visited my sister, saying you were with an American government agency. You were so reticent about it she thought you must be CIA. Was that fair?"

"I don't think we have to go into that," Quin began.

"Oh, yes. I think we do. That man came to the hospital today, and I tried to hide at the apartment, but he'd already been there. He's everywhere I go, Thomas. How does he know? Who is he?" Anne stopped before she asked who Thomas was and whom he worked for. Time for that later.

"It's Anne's life, Quin. We have to let her know what's going on."

"No security clearance."

"I won't need any when he kills me. And I think he's been here. A guy on a motorcycle with the same helmet he wears cut off my driver when I was leaving the last time. Were you here? I called you, but it went to voicemail. Were you down here the whole time I was in the lobby, scared out of my mind, afraid to move? Why did you involve me in this affair at Wainwright's? What was I, protective cover?"

"No, yes, partly. I needed to be able to explain a lengthy stay on the island and being with you was a welcome excuse."

He put his hand on Anne's, but she jerked away.

"Uh, can we leave the personal relations to personal time? What are we going to do now?" Quin asked.

"Tell Anne what's going on, and she'll help us."

"Yes, do. But don't count on my help with any shady CIA operation."

"Just listen." Thomas leaned towards her. "The Secretary of State has established a task force to investigate gunrunning from the USA to war zones around the world. I'm on it. Quin is CIA liaison. She's coming here to work with a joint Israeli-Palestinian peace initiative that has a real chance at establishing a two-country solution. I'm here to give the appearance of a business meeting to a top-secret visit. As far as the official calendar is concerned, she's going to Canada."

"Why Canada?"

"Because the American press will ignore a visit to Ottawa."

"And this Blanc?"

"We thought he was strictly contract, but he seems to have access to an organization. Which one, we don't know," said Quin.

"You don't know who the opposition is? What are the possibilities, besides the Palestinians and Israelis? I suppose gunrunners, gun manufacturers, security firms, terrorist organizations, the IRA... the list is endless. But why would any of these organizations have any interest in killing me? If they're so well-connected, they must know that I don't know anything. Why is this bastard trying to kill me?"

Anne's chair scrapped the terrace. She stood with her back to the two men. Beyond the pink sand, the long-tails danced above the waves. Free, she thought. She wanted to be free too. Behind her, Quin was talking.

"We think he's made it personal."

"Personal. I thought that before, but I don't know him. How could it be personal?" She turned away for the sea. "I haven't done anything to him."

"Yes, you have. He knows you can identify him. And you won't leave it alone."

Anne sat down again. Thomas reached his hand towards her but didn't touch her.

"Not only that," he said. "You escaped and made him look bad to his bosses."

"Do you think he's working alone here or that there is someone else?"

"We don't know."

"So all I have to do is stay hidden until he kills whomever it is and goes away?"

She could do that. She could hide wherever they put her and stay in her room and eat room service and watch television until the conference was over and he killed someone, or not.

"No," Quin said. "Our experience with him is that he'll come after you."

"I could go home."

"Same problem. You'd still be a loose end, and he would want the satisfaction of killing you."

Damn, she thought. What the hell was she going to do? The police believed her, maybe, but wanted her to stay, and her only allies were her family and a couple of spooks who lied to her. She drummed the table with her fists.

"What do you want me to do?" she asked, turning to Thomas.

"Before you were hurt, I wanted you to come out to the estate with me for the next event, poke around. You're the only one who can identify him by sight—"

"He's changed his appearance. Did I tell you that?" Anne said. "He has brown hair now. I don't know if he changed his eyes too, but I expect he has. He can't change his walk."

"All the more reason for you to be there," Thomas said.

"Can't I stay wherever the security feed is going?"

"You'd be more useful on the floor, where you can watch for the walk in the places the camera can't cover," Quin said. "He likely knows where those spots are."

"So he can get me when your people aren't watching."

"So you can see him before he kills anyone," Thomas said.

"When is this meeting?"

"Two days."

Chapter Twenty-Three

The whine of a leaf blower rose above the workday clamor of cars and sirens in the Vermont town of Culver's Mills. A young man, ears covered with orange headphones, focused it on the hundreds of maple leaves that blanketed the courtyard lawn like a red and gold quilt. Adam waved to him and received an answering waggle of the blower hose.

Adam walked on, past the heroic statue of the town's founder— automatically touching the toe for luck— and up the stairs to Lil's door. The diner stood diagonally across the square from the courthouse in an old stone building that led previous lives as a lumberman's office and a general store. It had been Lil's for fifty years now. Lil herself was long gone, but the place remained the same. Red vinyl seats in high-backed booths filled the space in front the windows on three sides. A white enamel counter, worn through to black in a few places, ran the length of the room. A polished nickel milkshake maker stood on one end of the counter and an espresso machine at the other. Adam took one of the black and chrome stools and said hello to the woman behind the counter.

"Hi, Adam. Usual?"

"No, I'm branching out since we went to Bermuda."

Let me have one of those fish on a bun and fries."

"Travel broadens. Congratulations on the engagement."

A hand smacked him on the shoulder, and its owner took the stool beside him. Ted Atkins was a reporter for the local newspaper. He'd saved Anne's life when her investigation into a murder led her too close to rapids in a local river. He'd saved his own life, too. His depression lifted, he stopped drinking and developed a relationship with Peg, the energetic blond behind the counter.

"My congrats too. What took you so long?"

"Wanted to be sure she'd say yes."

"Did you see Anne in Bermuda?"

Adam told Ted to about the deaths and the trouble Anne was having with the local cops and about the man she was convinced was looking for her and would kill her.

"What can I do?"

"Do you have any contacts left in the big city?"

Ted was a crime reporter in Boston before a family tragedy brought him to Culver's Mills and work on the local paper.

"A few. What do you need?"

"Who is this guy Blanc? Why he's targeting Anne? Who's he work for? Find out what you can about the other players. There's a guy called Chuck Wainwright. What business is he in?"

"What's this meeting in Bermuda?"

"Supposed to be a business meeting but there's a lot of security. I overheard a conversation at a restaurant that identified a guy at another table as an Israeli businessman, maybe a Mossad agent, attending it.

"I'll see what I can do."

Ted's contact in Boston didn't want to talk on the phone or by e-mail. A few hours later, Ted walked out of Logan airport in Boston, into the bright sunshine of a New England autumn. The cab took him to a run-down hotel he remembered from his days and alcohol-fogged nights on the Boston paper. In a booth against the end wall of the dark bar, his contact huddled over a drink. Ted slid in across from him, shook his hand and asked the hovering water for soda water.

"What's up?"

"I need some information on a guy you might know something about."

"Who's the guy?"

"They call him Blanc."

"Christ, I hope you're under his radar."

"Who is he?"

"What I hear, a hit man for the arms cartel."

"Arms cartel?"

"Come on, Ted. You haven't been out of it that long. You know these guys all work together. They have a stronger lobby than the NRA and a bigger budget." He was whispering now, leaning across the table, and watching the room.

"He's targeted a woman who was only a possible witness to murder."

"Did she get in his way?"

"I suppose you could say so. He kidnapped her and she escaped."

"She's lucky to be alive. He hates women, especially if they won't do what he wants. His wife and kid are in witness protection. He got a private detective on them. When Blanc found them, he took out one Marshall, but the other one got them away."

"Who's the detective? Why did Blanc trust him? Why did he work for Blanc?"

"Name's Daemon, Mike Daemon. Has an office downtown but word is he works for a major arms manufacturer."

"Daemon. You got anything else?"

"Nope."

"Thanks for your help."

The office was in a standard high-rise in downtown Boston. The nameplate read Daemon Securities Consultants.

When Ted asked to see her boss, the receptionist asked the usual questions and then said, "I must tell you that we aren't taking new clients."

"That's okay. We're old friends. I only need a few minutes."

"Ted, long time."

The detective reached across his desk to shake Ted's hand. He was the same slightly overweight, slightly too-short guy that Ted remembered. He'd hung around the same bars as the journalists, picking up scraps of information.

"Day. You've gone all upscale," Ted said, waving a hand to take in the leather furniture and view over Boston.

"Not too bad, not too bad. What brings you to Boston from Culver's Mills?"

"I need some information if you still think you owe me."

"Hey, some debts can't be paid. What do you need to know?"

"I heard you work for a weapons maker. I need to know about a guy called Chuck Wainwright."

"I got nothing." He drained his glass and raised a finger to the bartender.

"Nothing you can give me or nothing."

"Nothing."

"What about another one called Blanc?"

"What are you doing asking questions about that psycho? If he hears about it, you'll be on his list." His glass slipped, spilling a drop of scotch. He dabbed at it with the blue square of a cocktail napkin.

"Who's he work for? That's the payback, Day. I want to know about this guy."

"What I hear, he's free-lance or was. Meticulous. Hates women and likes to kill them. Maybe he has an organization behind him now."

"Why's he hate women?"

"Mother abandoned him to an abusive father. Girlfriends, a

string of them, broke off with him. He married, had a son and a daughter. She left, gave it up to the cops and went into witness protection with the kids."

"What I heard, you found them for him."

"Yeah, what you heard. From who?"

"The source says you work for a gun cartel."

Ted watched the other man's face, saw the blood drain, and waited for the lie.

"I work for myself. We're done here."

He stood up, put out his hand, shook Ted's and waited, standing, until Ted left.

Not too bad, Ted thought. He was on the next flight to Bermuda.

The pilot's report on the weather in Bermuda: a sunny day; temperature twenty-three degrees Celsius; winds from the South at forty knots. Hurricane Gertrude was still aiming at the Carolinas and expected to miss Bermuda.

"Hurricanes?" Ted said to his seat-mate, a Bermudian on his way home.

"Not to worry. They don't hit us very often; we're only twenty miles long and two miles wide."

The taxi stopped in front of a two-story, square-built house graced by a white porch and roof.

"Here you are," the cabbie said. "Crown Hill."

"What do you mean, Crown Hill?"

"The name of the house, man. Crown Hill."

The many windows, including an arched Palladian in the second story, looked like a security nightmare, but Ted supposed that the building enjoyed all the required security upgrades. The front door was narrow, a lantern on either side. A discreet plaque below one of them identified the consulate.

Strange name for an American consulate, Ted thought. Inside, he told the receptionist he was a visiting journalist and showed his card.

"I'd like to speak to the Consul-General, please."

"I'm afraid she's quite busy at the moment. I could give you an appointment on Monday."

"Monday will be too late. I want to talk to her about the meeting at the Wainwright estate."

"I'll see."

When she returned, she told him the Consul could give him five minutes.

"Mr. Atkins. What can your government do for you today?"

The consul, a blonde woman in her mid-forties, reached across the federal-style desk to shake his hand.

"I came to Bermuda to see if I could do anything for a friend of mine who's in some trouble here. She's a Canadian, so you might not have heard of her— Doctor Anne McPhail?"

"Oh, yes. The doctor who found that poor young man in the art gallery."

"I've some information I've dug up and now what I need are press credentials that will let me into that meeting at the Wainwright estate."

"Meeting?"

"Madame, I'm sure you must know about it. I know the Secretary of State is coming and I'd like to be at the press conference she gives after."

"You aren't a foreign correspondent?"

"No, but the people of Vermont have a right to know what's going on."

As it happened, Ted knew the Consul was from New Hampshire.

"So they do. But what does this have to do with the Canadian woman?"

"I'm not sure. I'm following my nose on this one."

"I'll see what I can do. Where are you staying?"

And that was that. Ted took a cab to the Hamilton Princess, checked in and called Anne.

"Anne, I'm following a lead on a story that Adam put me onto. I'd like to talk to you about it if you have a few minutes to meet."

"Downstairs in your hotel, in the restaurant? I could be there in half-an-hour."

Anne hadn't been in the Hamilton Princess since its refurbishment. The elegant old hotel, only seven stories, had overlooked Hamilton Harbor for at least a hundred and twenty-five years. The port-couchère opened to a dazzling, white marble foyer, furnished with eighteenth-century elegance. The theme of white paint and white marble carried on into the bar. Ted was sitting in a comfortable-looking wicker chair at a glass table in front of a pillar. He stood up and kissed Anne's cheek before she sat down in the chair opposite.

"So good to see you again, Ted. What brings you to Bermuda?"

"Same here. Sorry about your leg. I wanted to follow up on that meeting that's happening here this weekend. I've a contact in Boston who talked to me about someone you know— a guy with white hair and grey eyes?"

"Yes, I...yes."

Ted leaned across the small table.

"He's a real bad dude. He hates women, and he takes his rage out on them whenever he can. The pi he hired to track his wife owed me a favor and told me about him."

"Why does he hate women?"

"Abandonment by his mother, rejection by girlfriends and his wife, the usual excuses. Who the hell knows?" Ted stopped talking as the server came and took their orders.

"Somehow, I don't feel sorry for him. I saw the boy he killed, and I thought he was going to kill me, and he may yet. Who's he work for? Did you find out?"

"I was told he works for a gun cartel, but I haven't got any names yet. You?"

"Maybe Wainwright, or that man that works for him, John Malcolm. Did his name come up?"

A group of businessmen, one of them a tall blonde man, passed their table and sat down, a little out of earshot. Ted leaned forward across the table and lowered his voice.

"Nope. I know about Wainwright, though. I brought you information about his holdings as far as I could follow. Mostly gossip."

He took Anne's hand and pressed a USB stick into her palm.

"Thanks. I'm going to the reception this weekend."

"What takes you there? Is your brother-in-law a politician here?

"No, Thomas Beauchamp is taking me."

"What's his involvement?"

"He's a business acquaintance of Wainwright."

"I'll see what I can find out about this Malcolm."

"Be careful yourself. There seems to be a considerable organization behind this."

"Arms cartel?"

"This is all too much for me. What are we doing here anyway? I came for a vacation and now I'm attending international meetings, and strange assassins are chasing me." Ted reached across the table to hold Anne's restless hands.

"I'm coming to that meeting. I'll watch your back."

"And I'll have yours."

Chapter Twenty-Four

At least this building was accessible, thought Anne. She knew the way from her previous visit to the Land Registry Office, so she didn't stop at reception but took the elevator to the third floor. She introduced herself to the receptionist who took her to a computer terminal, explaining on the way that the most recent files were digitized, but older ones weren't.

"I need the latest transactions. I have everything from the past."

"Do you? Well done. Reconstruction of records is difficult, and there have been a lot of problems with this piece of ground, but I expect you realized that from your search the last time you were here."

"I didn't think you recognized me."

Anne looked up into the tall woman's face.

"Oh yes. Adrienne told us you were being stalked."

"Adrienne?"

"Adrienne Spottiswood. She's my daughter."

"She has a difficult job." Anne wondered what else Adrienne told her mother and if talking outside the job was one of the habits that got her in trouble with her bosses.

"Here's the latest transaction."

Anne looked at the names of the seller and buyer, recognizing one. She stowed the copy the archivist made for her, thanked her and left.

Anne could see Mrs Smith watching from the window. Moments later, she was sitting at the kitchen table, her file folder open, sorry she was to give Margaret bad news.

"I have to tell you that, although your ancestor did own property in the area of the Wainwright estate, it wasn't the estate itself, but the old factory further along the seafront. The government expropriated it, and the title was taken from your great-grandfather. I haven't found any record of payment to him."

"No, no. He didn't get money. My grandmother told me."

"He should have been paid, or should have received a new house, but if he did, I can't find it. Mr Wainwright bought the property last year."

"So Nathan was right. We'll never get anything that was stolen from our family."

"I don't see any way you can be compensated for that, short of a political solution."

"A political solution?"

"The government might respond to pressure from the community if you could organize the other descendants."

"The people had to take the money or be left with nothing."

"That's right. I didn't go far into the political side of things. I was only interested in the land your relative owned."

"Could you do that—look into the political side of things?"

Margaret poured some more tea, dribbling a little on her immaculate white tablecloth. When she didn't notice, Anne wiped it with her napkin.

"I don't think it would be to your advantage. I could explain all this to Mr Wainwright and his daughter. Your land was one of the last parcels taken, with no money exchanged. Mr Wainwright might feel obliged to pay you something."

"I don't want to beg."

"You won't have to. I'll do the explaining and the asking."

Anne's next stop, after she visited the clinic to have the surgeon replace her heavy plaster cast with a lightweight one of blue fiberglass, was Adrienne's office.

"What can I do for you, Anne?"

So she was still Anne. Good.

"I need to go to Vermont for a short visit, no more than two days. Up to now, you've told me I couldn't leave. That does that still hold?"

"We still need you as a witness."

"I know that. I need some information, and I need to talk to people in Vermont to get it."

"Phone lines and Internet down?"

"Not secure. Not enough for me, anyway. Whoever or whatever is behind this has more resources than you or I can imagine. So I want to go to Vermont. Are you going to allow it, or not?"

Adrienne took a Canadian passport from her desk drawer. She looked through it and placed it in the middle of blotter on her desk.

"Of course, you have family here."

"Yes."

"I'll allow it, but call me when you get back."

"I will."

Anne stopped at a travel agent to book a flight on the next plane out. She made it onto the plane, a struggle even with assistance from the airline. Five hours later she was sitting in an airport lounge in Newark, New Jersey, waiting for a flight to Burlington. Hours and hours. She hoped the information would be worth it. Adam said that Pete would meet her at the airport.

"Hi, Doctor McPhail. How was the trip?"

"Not too bad. How are you? Adam said you'd been shot again."

She took an appraising, professional look at his stocky frame. She knew he was the officer Adam depended upon the most.

"It wasn't much, but they have me on the desk for a while. Out of the office today, anyway."

"I'm glad to see you."

With that Anne put her head back and went to sleep.

"We're here, Doctor McPhail."

"All ready? That was a boring trip for you, Pete."

"Nah, just quiet. I brought you to Catherine's first.
That okay?"

"Yes, thanks."

The clapboard house with its welcoming porch still needed paint. Her friend Catherine Laporte ran it as a bed and breakfast but took guests only occasionally now. She returned to school when her twin boys went to university, and now she was halfway through a law degree. School trumped paint for Catherine.

"How long was your trip?" Catherine asked, after a hug.

"Long."

"Tea?"

"Please. And then I'd like to go to the station to see Brad."

"Brad? I thought you were coming to see Adam?"

"Him, too, but I need a computer genius, and Brad's the only one I know who's a police officer as well."

Beyond the windows in Catherine's cheerful kitchen, the garden held an early autumn profusion of oranges and reds and yellows, accented with an occasional splash of blue from Catherine's favorite butterfly bushes. Anne told Catherine about her days in Bermuda, skirting around the issue of why Thomas lied to her.

"So how do you feel about Thomas?"

"I don't know. He didn't exactly lie to me. He didn't share all of his life and I'm not sure I trust him anymore."

"Are you going to give him a chance?"

One thing about Catherine, she always got right down to it.

"I'll see. I can't tell you much about it, but he hasn't done anything wrong."

"He always seemed to be a good man."

"I'd better be going."

"I'll drive you."

Catherine stopped at the courthouse steps. Anne paused to look at the square, enjoying for a moment its postcard beauty before starting up the stone steps towards the oak door of the courthouse. The chips knocked out of the wall by shots fired at her on her first visit to Vermont were darker as pollution and time changed white to grey.

She crossed the foyer, pushed open another fine oak door and entered the workaday world of the police station. She paused at the desk to tell the receptionist she was there to see Brad.

"Welcome back, Doctor McPhail," the woman said. "Brad's at his desk."

"Thanks."

Anne maneuvered her way across the squad room. The cables that connected the computers still snaked from desk to desk, a maze of duct-tapped obstacles. Only the screen-savers provided splashes of color in an otherwise institutional-grey world.

"Doctor McPhail."

Brad bounded out of his chair, smiling all over his good-natured face, loomed over her and pumped her hand.

"I'm so glad to see you, Brad. How are you?"

"Great. I got married last month."

"Congratulations. I need your help, but I think I'd better go check in with the boss first."

"He's in the office."

Adam's blinds were closed, but the door was open. He'd been watching her progress across the squad room. Spottiswood let you go, did she? Or is there a warrant for your arrest?" he said after he hugged her.

"She let me go," Anne said, "but she did comment that I had family on the island."

"What do you need from Brad?"

"Information on the arms trade."

"The arms trade?"

"Yes. I want to know who the major players at the corporate

level are and how some of the people in Bermuda are involved, especially Wainwright. Do you think he can do that?"

"I asked Ted Atkins to get us that information, but I haven't heard back from him. I didn't want to risk an internet search tipping off Blanc or his bosses that you were still digging."

"Ted's in Bermuda. I don't think it matters. I know I'm still on Blanc's list, but I want information on Wainwright. I want to help Mrs Smith get compensation for the loss of her family's land, if not her son..." Anne's voice started to wobble, and she stopped talking.

"Let's ask".

Brad, would you help Anne find some information she needs?"

"No problem. What is it?"

"I'm interested in the arms trade and in particular the corporate structure of the major companies. If there's any way of finding out the same information about more closely held firms, I'd like that too."

"Who are you looking for?"

"A man called Charles Wainwright."

"People have talked about the military-industrial complex for years," Adam said. "The arms trade is bigger than one guy."

They stood behind Brad, watching him search databases.

Brad agreed. "Here's a list of the five major players. Lockheed Martin in the US, BAE Systems in Britain, Boeing, Northrup-Grumman, General Dynamics, all USA. Tough to say if one guy is heavily invested in any one or all of them."

"I think you'll find him further down the list, if at all. Maybe look for him shareholders lists, or attendees at shareholders meetings or tagged in photos with some of the directors of those five," Anne said.

"Do you mind telling me why we're looking."

"I think there's an organization running an assassin-for-hire and Wainwright may be involved."

Late in the day, Brad handed her a file with all he could find on Charles Wainwright.

"As far as I could look he's heavily invested in the arms trade, but not in any one company and not in any of the major US ones. He seems to spread the money around the world— German, Israeli, Japanese. He attends very few meetings and splits his time between Bermuda and New York."

"So no involvement in anything that looked like a cartel?"

"Not that I could find."

"That's useful information but won't help me pressure him into giving any compensation to Mrs Smith."

The next morning she was back in Bermuda and knocking on Thomas's door.

Chapter Twenty-Five

"I've been looking for you," Thomas said. "Spottiswood said not to worry, but she wouldn't say where you were."

The wind blowing off the sea rustled in the trees outside the villa. Anne opened the patio doors, letting the fresh sea air fill the room.

"I needed to go to Vermont."

"She let you leave the island?"

"Yes. She said something about my having family here."

Anne prowled around the room, stopping again to look out at sea.

"Did you take that as a threat? Would you like a drink?" He opened the minibar and took out a beer.

"No. Yes, white wine if there is any."

She stepped outside. When Thomas brought the wine, she sat down at the wrought-iron table. She wanted to ask him, to know for certain. Certain, that was if she could be sure his answer was the truth.

"Are you in business with Chuck Wainwright?"

"In business. No. We belong to some of the same organizations.

When I used to play golf, we made up a foursome occasionally." He looked surprised at the question.

"Who chose his estate for the meeting?"

"The CIA. Why are you asking about Wainwright? What did you find out?"

"Here, I found records for the property next to his. Wainwright bought it, but it belonged to Margaret's family until the nineteen twenties. In 1923 the last recorded person was dragged from her land and resettled, but not Noah Roberts. His land was expropriated—the minister signing the order was the developer's nephew—but there's no record of any payment, any new home. It was stolen. In the forties, it was used by the American government for interrogating Nazi spies."

"Who told you that?"

"My brother-in-law, who got it from his father. You know how things go in small places."

"That's got nothing to do with the meeting."

"No."

Anne put down her glass and closed her eyes. God, she was tired. All that traveling.

"What else?"

Thomas was restless. He walked to the corner of the villa and looked up the hill towards the hotel proper and then out along the beach.

"I went to Vermont to ask Brad—you know, the police officer who's great with computers—to help find out who owned what. Wainwright's a major player in the arms industry. He and others have no market if peace breaks out. Didn't you say there was a good chance of success here?"

"Not good enough to affect that business."

"What about your special investigations? What if they want to shut her up and shut your group down?"

"Paranoia?"

"I don't think so. The resources behind Blanc are formidable, as good as the CIA."

"Have you decided to help us?"

"If we could have a little chat with Wainwright about Margaret and her property."

"After the SecState leaves."

"All right. It can wait until after."

"Anne, what about us?"

She looked across the table, into his dark eyes and then beyond him to the sea.

"I've had a few hours to think about that, hanging about hospitals and airports the way I've been. I don't want to know what you do for the CIA, or what you used to do, but I'll help you with the meeting this weekend, and then we'll see how it goes."

"We'll see how it goes."

They sat, silent, drinking wine and watching the waves spill onto the shore.

Chapter Twenty-Six

Blanc stroked the barrel of his Jericho before tucking into the waistband of the polyester pants, under his shirt where he could feel the cold steel against the small of his back. He arranged a bow tie to miss his Adam's apple and buttoned up the waiter's jacket to complete the uniform. He ran his hand through his hair. Soon time to revert to white, he thought; the roots were beginning to show. The television behind him, tuned to a weather station, repeated its hurricane warning. He needed to get this done before the hurricane arrived. But he had at least another day, according to the forecast. He switched it off before the revised update that would have cut that time in half.

He put the identification taken from the dead waiter, a new hire, into the pocket of his raincoat — the controller would have to agree that this death was not random but necessary — buttoned up the coat, took one last look and sauntered out the door. Time to join the bus that was taking the waiters out to the estate.

The bus turned into the rain-slicked driveway at the Wainwright estate and drove up the hill to the kitchen entrance to the house, in front of the five-car garage where security would screen the waiters. A narrow alley ran between the house and the garage. The melee of waiters occupied the guards, and he slipped into the alley, left his raincoat behind a row of trash cans and walked onto the terrace looking like a waiter giving a discreet tug to his jacket.

He took a tray of filled champagne glasses from the bar.

"Where are the rest of your guys?" the bartender asked. "They're getting thirsty."

"Security's slow."

He edged into the crowd, rapidly lost the contents of his tray and returned for a refill. Other waiters appeared, and he moved to the periphery of the crowd.

Gawkers crowded the wide double doors that would open in moments for the Secretary of State and her entourage. A dais stood at one end of the room, fronted by microphones. He took a position with the sight line he needed, near his chosen exit.

The doors opened; the Secretary, all smiles, shook the hands reaching out to her on her way to the dais. The Secret Service detail —some of it— moved into the room ahead of and beside her. Two stood back by the door, scanning the room. Blanc reached for his gun and waited for the moment when she would begin to speak when all eyes would be on her, and he could fire, and disappear.

Chapter Twenty-Seven

Anne pulled the pant leg of her black silk suit over her new blue cast. She smoothed the neck of the deep pink shirt she wore with it, so that it sat on the lapels of the long coat. The tiny receiver Thomas gave her disappeared into her ear canal, and she clipped on the microphone, hidden in a diamond brooch on her left shoulder. It was a shame, she thought, to spoil the effect with crutches.

"How lovely you look," said Thomas.

"Thanks. Is it time?"

"Yes. Are you okay with this?"

"No. I'm scared," she said.

"Quin will be watching the monitors. I'll come in with the Secretary."

"The areas with no cameras worry me. He knows where the blank spaces are."

"And you know what he looks like."

The limousine met them under the portico and whisked them through the downpour to the estate. Anne kept her face to the window, watching the morning glories that wound around every pole and wire bend their lovely sky-blue heads in the deluge. The hurricane would tear some of the tendrils from the wires, but the plants would prevail, twisting around the poles again in their search for the sun.

"What do you have to do?" she asked.

"I have to speak to Quin, join the Secretary's Secret Service detail for a briefing on the storm and come back into the ballroom. It should only take a few minutes. The meeting is over now; they're mingling and having a glass or two before she makes an announcement.

"Will we be late?"

"No. She has half-an-hour. She always wants a little time to put the last touches on her remarks and her makeup."

"Is she flying out before the hurricane?"

"They all are if the storm doesn't change direction or speed."

Ted called his paper before going out to the Wainwright estate.

"Ted, good to hear from you," boomed his editor. "What's happening in Bermuda?"

"Hurricane on its way; Secretary of State is here for a meeting when she's supposed to be in Canada; Mossad and CIA agents in town, and I suppose Secret Service too; an apparent hit man on the loose: this is a great place.

"When can you file?"

"After the meeting tonight. I can't promise that there won't be transmission problems with the hurricane, but I'll try to get to you as soon as I can."

"So don't hold the front page?"

"Yes, don't hold it.'"

Ted walked into the ballroom, impressed by it in spite of his long experience covering everything from local student proms to the Inauguration. He noted the positions of the microphones, and then looked for Anne and Thomas. He watched Thomas leave Anne.

He noticed a waiter who was moving against the crowd, edging towards a door across from the microphones. Anne was on the move, too.

Chapter Twenty-Eight

The ballroom was filling up with people and was reaching that stage of a party when people start to shout to be heard. Most of them were holding glasses. Anne noticed one waiter, with the hair color she was watching for, slide around the room with his tray of champagne balanced at his shoulder. He returned for a refill, loaded more glasses on his tray and was last in a bevvy of other waiters.

Anne stood as tall as she could and craned her neck, trying to see over the crowd. She would have to move around the room to the dead spaces, where the security cameras didn't penetrate. The Secretary was going to say her few words at the dais at one end of the room. People started to move towards it, most of them with press passes clipped to their jackets.

"How ya doing," said Quin's voice in her ear.

"I'm too short. Have you seen him?"

"No."

She'd seen Blanc kill once. He'd chosen to be near a door, for a quick exit. Perhaps he always did. She knew that, besides the grand double doors that led into the supper room that was being used for the conference, there were three ways out of the room. French doors opened onto the terrace, but escape would be difficult into the storm. Another, a swinging door, led to a service area. Across the room, the third door accessed a hallway leading to the family living room. That would be the one he chose, she thought and started into the crowd. The crowd moved of her way, some of it looking annoyed at the crutches. She heard a woman whisper that she would have stayed home if her leg were broken.

Her, too. She wanted to stay home too.

Ahead, the people edged towards the opening doors, all eyes on the secretary, hands reaching out to her as she paused to speak to an acquaintance or pat a shoulder or receive a hug.

A tall blond man seemed to drift in the same direction she was. She was closer. Through the gap the crowd left as it parted for her, she saw Blanc, his weapon held down and behind him.

He was waiting, she thought, waiting for the Secretary to speak when she would be on the dais when everyone would be looking at her, and he could fire over their heads. He hadn't seen Anne yet, but she would have only a moment.

She took her weight on her left crutch and her protesting leg, brought the right crutch up and under Blanc's arm.

"Gun. Gun," she yelled.

The bullet buried itself in the ceiling, dropping a rain of plaster. Blanc gave Anne one venomous look and fled. The door crashed behind him.

Ted was there. He picked her up and recovered her crutch, waited until she balanced and walked with her to the living room.

"He went this way, Ted."

"You can be sure he won't be coming back."

Moments later Thomas came, and Ted sprinted from the room, saying, "Anne, I'm going to file."

Thomas crouched beside her chair.

"I have to go. Will you be all right?"

Blanc swiveled, ran through the door and turned the lock behind him. He forced himself to slow down, turned a corner into the kitchen and asked a nearby chef for water.

"Over there," the chef said and waved him down the room.

Blanc took a glass from one counter, filled it at a sink halfway along and reached the end of the kitchen without drawing any attention from staff. He stepped outside, took a pack of cigarettes from his pocket and lit one. He waited, smoking slowly, standing beside the trash cans.

"Did you see anyone run through here?"

"No, man. I been smoking all alone."

The guard rushed past and into the garage. Blanc stepped on the butt and moved down the alleyway towards the terrace. He knew that across the terrace lay the path to the sea the woman had taken. He would decide what to do with her later.

The terrace was deserted. The heavy rain on the side of the terrace exposed to the sea fell in dense sheets slanting in front of the wind and hid him from those inside. He crossed the terrace and turned a corner. He could see into the house, the living room, where a woman, that woman, sat huddled into a chair. Maybe he should deal with her now.

"Blanc."

The voice came from behind him. He turned to face the controller.

"Help me get out of here," Blanc yelled against the wind.

"Of course."

Chapter Twenty-Nine

Anne sat in the living room. At least she supposed Wainwright called it that, furnished as it was with seven-foot sofas covered in fabric that mimicked the garden, vast summer rugs in shades of cream and blue, airy drapes that fluttered in the wind seeping under the doors. Beyond the doors, the rain blurred the garden to shades of black.

She wished that Thomas would come and take her back to Liz before the wind made it impossible to drive. But he was still somewhere, searching for the shooter. A man lurched onto the terrace, yelling back at someone closer to the house. One of the searchers? She peered through the rain-soaked window, straining to hear the voices but all she heard was an explosion of sound that could have been a branch, breaking. The man on the terrace staggered and then fell onto the stones. She pushed against the wind to open the French doors and struggled across the rain-slicked terrace to reach him. He was dead; his hair, beginning to show its white roots, was plastered against his scalp; rain streamed off the clouding corneas of the grey eyes. She closed them.

"Doctor McPhail."

She turned and saw Malcolm standing behind her. His suit,

ruined by the downpour, clung to him; his hair, blown back from his face gave him the look of a CNN reporter, in a television spot from yet another Florida hurricane.

"You'd better come back in the house."

"Yes, but who did this?"

"I'll look after this Blanc. Come in before the storm gets worse."

He helped her with her crutches and walked her back to the living room. He brought her a drink— rum and lemon and hot water— and a blanket closed the drapes and left her there.

She closed her eyes, letting the warmth from the hot toddy take away some of the horrors. She opened them again. She felt exposed, all alone in one corner of the vast space. The library, she thought. It was beyond the door on the opposite side of the room. Perhaps other people were there. She navigated the thick pile of the rug, leaving her drink behind. She closed the library door behind her but thought she heard an echo, perhaps another door closing, somewhere behind her. She sat on a soft chair in a corner near the fireplace. A fire would be good, even if the comforting crackles were lost in the distorting sound of the wind. She heard Malcolm swearing in the other room when he didn't find her there. He must be shouting, she thought. What was that about? She started to call to him but stopped. What was he doing on the terrace, in the rain?

The wind raced in from the sea, pushing the surf ahead of it, up and over the cliffs at the edge of the estate. The elderly trees forming the border of the gardens bowed before it and here and there a limb, weakened from age or disease, splintered and fell. Lightening struck and left the house in darkness.

"Quin," she said. "Quin."

No answer. The power must have knocked out their communications. Anne cowered in her chair, trying to remember how many doors there were, and whether or not she was close to them. He could have come in without her hearing. The wind and the thunder and the thudding rain on the roof silenced any noise of his passage.

What was in the library? The day they escaped from the warehouse, Wainwright brought them here. Bookshelves all round, she remembered, and a vast desk that dominated it all. Where there was a desk, there might be a paper-knife or even a gun in a drawer. Perhaps Wainwright was a man who liked to own weapons as well as build them?

She inched along the bookshelves, one careful step after another until she felt the desk with her hip. Maybe he couldn't hear her. Maybe the desk was so perfect that the drawers would open quietly. Wainwright was left- handed. Surely, if there were anything he would need in a hurry, he would keep it on the left side of the desk. She held her breath, tugged at the handle of the top drawer, breathed again as it slid out silently towards her.

Nothing. Why would a man have such a desk and keep nothing in it? She nudged the chair aside, knelt on the floor and felt inside the kneehole. Near the top, she felt leather and then steel. She pulled the gun from the holster and explored it with fingers that seemed to belong to someone else. A switch moved, but did she take the safety off or put it on? Would Wainwright have kept a gun here, ready to use, but needing that extra second. She moved the switch back into position.

"I can hear you breathing," he said. "I'm coming for you."

Why was he terrorizing her? Why didn't he get it over with? Blanc was dead, their operation in shambles. Why didn't he go away? What did he think she knew? She felt the back and sides of the kneehole, backed in and faced the opening. She put her finger on the trigger of the gun, steadied her shaking right arm and waited, sipping air that smelled of dust and leather and oil.

What did she know? Blanc was dead. He killed the boy and Jasmine and tried to kill her. He failed in his attempt to kill the Secretary. Who killed him?

She remembered the body, the white skin of his face stark against the black stones of the terrace. Malcolm found her there. What did he say?

Go inside; I'll take care of this Blanc.

Blanc. How did he know it was Blanc, or rather how did he know she would? Thomas said Malcolm wasn't part of the operation, so how did he know?

That was why he needed to kill her. She could place him on the terrace at the time of the murder. How would he explain her death?

"You won't suffer," he said, his voice a whisper, so close she expected his face to swim out of the darkness in front of her. "I'll take you to the sea. They say it's a painless death, slipping under the water. Come out, so I can give you to the sea."

Would she be able to see the difference in the dark when he looked under the desk? Would she know he was there before he yanked her from her hiding place? A light flashed somewhere. Oh, God, a flashlight. He would be able to see her. But she could see the light.

She would know where he was, first. But was he right-handed or left-handed? She tried to remember, thinking of him handing her a drink or her coat. Right. He was right-handed. That meant she could aim to the left of the light. No. If he held a gun or a knife he would have that in his right and the flashlight in his left. What if he meant to strangle her or beat her to death? Then it would be in his right.

Choose, Choose. His left. He wouldn't come in there without a weapon. She moved to the front of the kneehole. Now she could see the light flashing around the room, searching for her in the corners. He was still far away but coming towards her. She pointed the gun to the right of the light and squeezed the trigger. The recoil sent her crashing back into the chair. It rolled away from her, leaving her floundering on the carpet. The sound of the shot echoed around the kneehole and then around the room; pain exploded in her ears; an acrid smell, cordite, she supposed, filled her nostrils.

There was silence. What happened to her hearing? Had the pain been her eardrums bursting? Where was he? Was he dead? Why wasn't anyone coming? She crept under the desk, pointed the gun at the darkness and waited.

A door crashed from its frame; light flashed around the room; voices called her name and Malcolm's.

"Here's Malcolm. He's been shot."

That was Wainwright.

"Anne. Annie, Where are you?"

Thomas. That was Thomas. But she couldn't speak. She huddled in her little cave, still pointing the gun. A light blinded her. A voice, Thomas's voice said, "It's all over, Annie. Give me the gun. Take your finger off the trigger and give me the gun."

"He's still out there."

"No, he's dead. You're all right now. Give me the gun." She dropped the gun on the soft rug and crept out.

Thomas lifted her up and she clung to him. "It's all over," he said again.

Chapter Thirty

Thomas and Quin met Adrienne at the door. "Again, Mr Beauchamp. This time, I understand she admits to pulling the trigger."

"Please, come with us," Quin said, displaying his credentials.

They sat in an office furnished with leather chairs, an eighteenth century desk and banks of computer monitors, watching the playback of the attempted assassination.

"You don't have film of him pulling his gun, only Anne's word?"

"We have another witness."

Thomas went to the door and called Ted.

"Detective-Inspector Spottiswood, Ted Atkins. Ted is a reporter from Vermont and a friend of Anne's. He wasn't close enough to stop Blanc, but close enough to see what was happening."

Ted told her about seeing Blanc take his gun from his belt and raise it, only to be hit by Anne's metal crutch. Ted stopped to help her, so he didn't see where Blanc went. He only knew he disappeared through the exit door.

"You're a good friend of Doctor McPhail's," she began.

"Yes, and before you ask, I haven't talked to her since we left her in the living room and I went to file the story. And I wouldn't lie to protect a killer, even if she were my friend."

"Is Anne a CIA operative?"

"No," said Quin. "She isn't."

"She's who she says she is and she's only involved in this because of me and our relationship. If the gun she held killed Malcolm, and I doubt it did, she fired in self-defense."

"She didn't see a gun—"

"He was threatening her, and she's on crutches with a broken leg. What else could she do? Come on, Adrienne. You've talked to her and tracked her every move. You know she isn't a killer. That gun only fired once. Who fired the second shot?"

"You're both armed?"

"No, not me," Thomas said.

"Of course," Quin said. He offered her his gun.

Adrienne took it, smelled it, checked the clip and returned it. She knew he'd been authorized to carry it concealed.

"I'll talk to her."

"Remember she saved the Secretary's life. They'll probably want to give her a medal."

"So don't arrest a hero?"

"Something like that."

Wrapped in a blanket and wearing a too-long set of hospital greens, Anne huddled in a chair in the living room watching the progression of police, and others she presumed were crime-scene investigators. One of them came for her.

"We need your fingerprints and your clothes, Doctor McPhail and we need to swab your hands and arms."

"Why? I told you I fired a gun at that man or at least fired to where I thought he was. And you already have my fingerprints."

"We know that, but we have to follow procedure. If you would come with me."

Then she waited. Sooner or later, Adrienne would come, and she would be arrested and spend the rest of her life on this godforsaken island, waiting for the occasional visit from her sister. Thomas and Quin came by, patted her arms, one each, and told her not to worry. Best not call the solicitor yet, they said. Let them talk to Adrienne first.

She closed her eyes and drifted off, waking with a scream as she fired the gun again, saw those dead eyes staring at her. The detective sat beside her.

"Adrienne."

"Yes. Are you awake enough to talk to me?"

"Yes."

"Tell me."

She hadn't warned her. Maybe she would have to go over it all again somewhere else. She told the story, from arriving at the party to seeing Blanc raise the gun to watching him die in the rain, to hearing Malcolm.

"What did he say?"

"He said he would give me to the sea."

"How many shots did you fire?"

"One, I think. The recoil sent me back against the chair and I couldn't see the light anymore."

"One shot shattered a mirror; a second killed him.

"Are you sure about how many times you fire?"

"I pulled the trigger only once. What kind of gun is it? Is it the kind that shoots many bullets with one pull?"

"No, an ordinary pistol."

"Then I don't understand."

"Nor do I. The bullet we recovered from the wall behind the mirror was from that gun. We're waiting to hear what was in the body."

Anne leaned back and closed her eyes, but Adrienne was still there when she opened them.

"Have they taken them away?"

"Them?"

"I told you, didn't I? Blanc was dead, out there, on the terrace."

"There was no body on the terrace."

"He must have dumped it into the sea. That's what he said: "I'll take care of this Blanc"."

"We'll check Malcolm's body for other DNA. Eric," she called.

"Yes, ma'am."

"Send someone to the shore. We're looking for the body of a white male, with dark hair, white at the roots."

"The storm," Anne said.

"We can only look."

"Are you going to arrest me?"

"No, I've had a chat with Thomas Beauchamp and Quin Randall. It appears you're a hero. You saved the Secretary's life."

Later, Anne stood at the window.

"Are you coming back to the hotel with me?"

Only the broken and uprooted trees, the hedges stripped of their flowers, the shattered blossoms scattered across the driveway remained as evidence of the storm's passage. Shards of blue appeared among the still-black clouds scudding across the sky. Anne turned from the window to answer Thomas.

"Not this morning. I want to go to my sister's. She'll be worried, and I haven't been able to reach her on the phone. I suppose the lines are down and the cell service too."

"Only satellite phones are working. When will I see you again?"

"You said you would set up a meeting so that I could talk to Wainwright about Mrs Smith."

"That's not what I meant."

"I know, but I have to finish with this island before I can move on to us."

"I'll set it up, but it may be soon. He said something about leaving."

"Sooner suits me fine. I need to go home."

Ten hours later, Liz knocked on the door of Anne's bedroom and came in with coffee and a message.

"I'm sorry to wake you, but Thomas insisted I give you this message right away."

"What is it?"

"The meeting is at seven this evening. He said he would pick you up at quarter to."

"What time is it now?"

"Five."

Anne's eyes filled with tears and her voice came in a tight whisper.

"Every time I go to sleep, I wake up with the sound of that gun going off. I killed a man, Liz. When they turned on the lights, and I crawled out of that hole, I saw his dead eyes accusing me."

Liz sat on the bed beside Anne and put her arms around her while she sobbed.

"You had no choice."

"I know, but that doesn't take away this horrible echo in my head."

"Do you want to cancel this meeting?"

"No. I want to talk to Ted Atkins. Are the phones working? He's at the Hamilton Princess."

Ted was at the hotel and then at their front door. "Have you been able to find out anything more,"

Anne asked.

"I called my source in Boston last night. He couldn't add anything about Blanc or Wainwright. Malcolm is still a mystery. No one seems to know who he worked for, likely not himself. The accident that killed Wainwright's butler was likely arranged, and then Malcolm met Wainwright and got the job as his replacement. Blanc made a few calls to Switzerland while he was on the island, so Quin told me, but who answered is still unknown. Out of service now."

"Why did he kill Nathan Smith? Surely there were easier ways to get onto the estate?"

"Blanc liked killing."

The flat statement started Anne shaking again. Ted reached out a hand to her shoulder.

"Are you staying on the island?"

"No, my flight's at seven. Give me a call when you get back to Canada, will you?"

Anne said good-bye and came back into the kitchen. "Adrienne called. She said she would be here in five

minutes." Liz's voice broke into a harsh sob. "Did she say she was coming to arrest me?"

"No."

Chapter Thirty-One

Adrienne walked into her apartment, took off her jacket, shrugged out of the vest underneath and sank into the welcoming depths of her only armchair. The space was tiny, but it was all hers, a refuge from the chaos at work and questions at her mother's. What a mess the case turned into. What was it going to mean for her career? She wanted to leave Bermuda, to rack up experience somewhere else, to learn different methods of detection and have access to more advanced forensics. But she was stuck here, so it seemed.

The doorbell rang.

"Hi. Can I come in?" Paula stood on the doorstep, holding a bottle of wine.

"What do you want?"

"Just to drink a congratulatory glass of wine with you." She waggled the bottle.

"You might as well come in."

Paula walked across to the two kitchen cabinets, sink and microwave that served as a kitchen, took two glasses out, twisted the cap from the bottle and poured the wine. "Congratulations.

Case closed," she said, lifting a glass towards Adrienne. "Isn't it? Why so glum?"

"Forensics showed the second bullet, the kill shot, came from a different gun. One of the agents was armed—it wasn't his gun—the other wasn't armed, and Wainwright had time to get rid of one. So no, the case isn't closed, but I have no clue where to look for a killer."

"Who else was in the house?"

"At least two hundred people, in a hurricane, after an assassination attempt, including the CIA, reporters from the US, assorted secret service from several countries, many with diplomatic immunity."

"What secret service?"

"American, British, Palestinian, Mossad..."

"What does your boss say?"

"I can't tell you that."

"Off the record."

"Case closed."

"Did you say Mossad?"

"So I heard out there."

"Any clue which one he was?"

"None."

"So a dead end?"

"Yes."

Thomas sat on the windy terrace. Beyond the beach, the surf pounded the surf under the cloud-darkened sky. Quin came around the corner of the villa. A man with him, blond and burly in contrast to Quin's slim dark build, stood back a little.

"Tom."

"Quin. Who's this?"

"Ari."

"Ari what?"

"Ari's enough. We need to talk."

Later, in the lobby of the hotel, they said good-bye to Ari.

"I have to go too," said Quin.

Thomas nodded towards the parking lot. Adrienne stood by her car.

"Gentlemen, I have to talk to you."

"Not here."

They drove in her car, parked at a nearby beach and listened.

"I don't want to get in the way," she said. "I need to know if I can close the book on Malcolm and be satisfied that he was killed by someone saving Anne's life."

"Yes," said Quin.

"Good. I also need a favor. This case has taught me a lot about myself, and I think I'm a better cop now. I want out of this police force, off this island and some police work to do that is more than picking up drug-users and gangbangers. I think one or both of you can help me with that."

"What's your citizenship?"

"Bermudian and British."

"Would London suit you?" Quin asked.

"Yes."

"Leave it with me."

She dropped them back at the hotel.

"What can you do for her?

"Training program in the UK. After that, she's on her own."

"You see something in her?"

"She's dogged, and she's more flexible than she seemed. She's intelligent."

"Always good to have a contact in Britain."

"That too."

* * *

"Adrienne's here," Liz said.

"Why now?" Anne said.

Adrienne paused at the foot of the stairs leading up to the door, then held the railing as she climbed.

"She looks so tired," Anne said. "She looks like I feel."

"Don't have too much sympathy. Remember what she put you through."

Adrienne chose the only straight-backed chair in the room, facing away from the window and towards Liz and Anne who sat together on the sofa. That was a cop's habit, thought Anne. Adam did the same thing, always facing the exit or sitting where the light would fall on whomever he was talking to.

"So?" Anne said.

"We have the forensics back. Your gun—"

"Not my gun."

"Not your gun. The gun you fired was not the gun that killed Malcolm."

"I didn't kill him? You're sure."

"Yes."

Anne collapsed forward. Sobs, muffled by her hands, shook her body. Liz put her arms around her and held her until she was quiet.

"I didn't know how I was going to face it."

"Face what?"

"Being a killer. All my life has been about healing. I didn't know that I would kill someone, or try to, to save my own life."

"None of us knows until we have to choose," Adrienne said.

"Now, I have to live, knowing that about myself."

Chapter Thirty-Two

Anne sat in the kitchen, picking apart an oatmeal muffin while she waited for Thomas and Quin.

"You could have said you wanted dinner first," Liz said.

"But I didn't. I wanted to get this over with."

When they arrived, Anne waved them into chairs. "Help yourselves to muffins," she said.

"Has Adrienne told you that the gun you fired didn't kill Malcolm?"

"Yes, she came."

"We need to know what you're going to say to Wainwright," Thomas said.

"Why?"

"You can't accuse him of murder, not in front of witnesses," Quin said.

"I don't intend to. I want money for Mrs Smith, and I think he owes some to her. He may think the alternative is an investigation into his activities, but I won't say so. You, on the other hand, may be able to imply that by being with me."

"Getting close to blackmail, aren't you?" Quin asked.

"Not at all. I don't intend to threaten him with anything, but he knows I have friends who are CIA and police and press. He may feel a little impetus to settle and hope it all goes away."

"What about Ted Atkins. Did you ask him to come?"

"No."

"And that other reporter, Paula."

"No, again."

"Spottiswood?"

"She came earlier. You know I get it that you want it kept quiet so that you can get along with your arms investigation. My goals are very simple: some justice for Mrs Smith—and we can tell her who killed her son— and some financial security for her; and for me, getting off this damn island."

"Then we'd better go," Thomas said.

The Wainwright house seemed deserted without its mob of security and caterers and diplomats. A two-man crew was working on the lawn, gathering fallen branches and returning garden furniture. A woman answered the door. Wainwright hadn't time to get himself a new butler, Anne thought. He'd be more careful next time.

"They're waiting for you in the sitting room."

Chuck Wainwright, Candice and a man that Anne assumed was a lawyer, introduced only as David Munroe, waited for them. Anne fled this room after Blanc was shot, taking refuge in the library next door. Then it had been vast and dark and full of the noise of the advancing hurricane. Now, with the sun streaming in through the open French doors and the winds reduced to a gentle on-shore breeze, it was inviting, a casual space filled with chintz-covered furniture and polished side-tables.

Candice hugged Anne. Wainwright and the lawyer stood until Anne sat, then took places the sofa opposite. Thomas and Quin stood by the fireplace, leaving Anne, or so she felt, to face them alone.

"What's this all about," Wainwright demanded.

"I have a story to tell you and a suggestion for you. Ninety years ago now, in the twenties, the government of the day, comprising white landowners, decided that the inland needed more American tourists, rich American tourists. To do that, they decided to build an exclusive enclave, with golf courses, clubhouses and lots to accommodate houses that could compete with Newport Beach, in the US.

But people lived on the land, poor black people with a community and deep roots. Mattered not. Expropriations went ahead; people were moved, most of them receiving houses elsewhere or money in return. They weren't happy, but they weren't homeless. In the last recorded event authorities evicted a woman from her home in front of the demolition crew."

Anne paused, but Wainwright said nothing, although the lawyer started taking notes. Candice, curled at one end of the sofa, looked away from Anne, out towards the lawn and the sea.

"That was the last recorded person. However, I found another, whose land was taken, expropriated by an order-in-council, signed by the developer's nephew. Citizens wrote outraged letters to the Gazette, but the expropriation was carried out. There is no record anywhere of Noah Roberts, the landowner getting land or money in exchange for his loss. The story came down through his family, but the details of the land were lost. Mrs Smith and Nathan believed this land, yours, was the lot that was stolen from Noah."

"Too long ago," the lawyer said.

"I don't think so. I've spent some time in the archives and the land registry office, searching the records. I found Noah's land but this," Anne waved her hand around to take in the house and the property, "wasn't it."

"You shouldn't have wasted your time. Munroe here searched before I bought this place."

"Did he search before you bought the old factory?"

Wainwright turned to the lawyer. "Well?"

"No need. The facts were all before the court."

"Not all the facts," said Anne. "That land belonged to Noah Roberts, and neither he nor his heirs were ever compensated."

"Nothing to do with me."

"No?

The Americans interrogated German prisoners there during the war, and Blanc used it to stash his hostages. He had keys, the locks were new, and the hinges were oiled. So it was used for criminal activity including an assault on me.

Children had played there over the years, including your daughter, my nephew and the little ones who helped me when I was pushed. The building is a dangerous, unsecured trap and you're responsible for it."

"And you were trespassing. Is that what this is, you want to sue me for your injuries?"

"Pay attention, Mr Wainwright. I started this story by telling you about Noah Roberts. It's his family that I think you owe compensation to, for the land that was stolen and the life that was taken. You have a significant investment in the arms trade."

Candice sat up and turned to look at her father. He focused on Anne.

"Blanc worked for someone with interest in fomenting conflict and putting the Secretary of State and her committee out of business."

"Guilt by association?" the lawyer scoffed.

"How closely do you want us to look?" Quin asked.

"What do you want?" Wainwright asked Thomas.

"Listen to Anne."

Anne went on, "I want you to write a letter to Mrs Smith, telling her that the land was stolen from her family, and offering her two million dollars in recompense."

"Two million!" Wainwright said.

"Don't be absurd," the lawyer added.

"Shut up, Mr Monroe," said Candice. "Dad, Nathan died because of the arms trade and you bringing this meeting to our home. The land was stolen from his family. Two million is much less that what you were going to spend for that Corot last month and it was likely a fake. I want you to give it to Mrs Smith. You owe her."

Wainwright looked from his daughter's tearful face to Anne's implacable one.

"All right," he said.

"Write the check," said Anne.

Chapter Thirty-Three

The overnight rains, remnants of the hurricane, washed the streets and the morning sunshine that followed dried the blossoms on the oleanders. Anne helped Liz clear the plates from the table in the garden before packing her last few items in her suitcase.

"I heard that Wainwright offered to fly you home." Liz sat on the bed, watching Anne fold and arrange her clothes.

"Yes, he did. But I want nothing to do with that man. I think he's involved with the organization that tried to kill the Secretary."

"Do Thomas and Quin think that too?"

"I don't think so. Adam does. It was his office that got the information for me."

"Just because he has shares in companies that make guns doesn't mean that he stirs up wars to sell them."

"Maybe not, but I'm not flying on his plane."

"I'll drive you to the airport."

"No thanks. Thomas is coming for me."

"That's on again, is it?"

"I don't know." Anne sat beside Liz on the bed. "He thinks I need some therapy for the shooting, and I do, but I'm not even sure an ordinary therapist can help me. I've got to live with this new person who would kill another to save her own life. Is that who I am?"

"An existential problem?"

"Perhaps. At any rate, we're on a WestJet flight to Toronto."

"What about the check for Mrs Smith?"

"We stopped by and gave it to her last night. Quill will take her to the bank this morning. He's going to help her set it up, so she gets a good income from it."

"What are you going to do?"

"Go home, clean my garden for fall, go to Spain."

"Spain?"

"I've never been there, and I've always wanted to go to Madrid to see Picasso's painting, Guernica."

"Spain in October. I hope it's peaceful."

"Me, too."

Anne watched the islands recede, become an emerald crescent, dotted with white rooftops, surrounded by the turquoise sea.

"Will you ever come back?" Thomas asked.

"Of course. My family is here, all that I have."

"You have me."

"We have to see how that goes. Let's talk about it later, at home, where I'm safe and strange men with weird eyes aren't trying to kill me."

"It's over. Try to get some rest."

She woke an hour later. Thomas was out of his seat, standing against the bulkhead, talking to a man in the front seat.

"I owe you one," she heard Thomas say. When he stood up to shake Thomas's hand, she recognized the blond man who had moved towards Blanc in the ballroom.

"Is that another business acquaintance?"

"Not my usual business. He's catching a flight from Toronto to Tel Aviv."

"What's his name?"

"Ari."

Ari, she thought. Now she knew who saved her life in that fear-filled room. Ari. She owed him one, too.

About the Author

Virginia Winters was born in Arnprior, Ontario, Canada and raised in the Ottawa Valley. After high school in Renfrew, another Valley town, she went down to Queens to study medicine, graduating in 1970. Fellowship in Pediatrics followed, with graduation in 1976. That year she and her husband, internist George Winters, moved to Lindsay, Ontario with their two children, and have lived there ever since. Virginia's interests, besides writing, are genealogy, gardening, photography, and studying languages (currently Spanish). The Face-painter Murders is the second in the Dangerous Journeys series.

Murderous Roots, Virginia Winters's first novel, an e-book, was published on December 1, 2009 by Write Words Inc. and is now available in paper and as an e-book at Amazon.com and other fine retailers.

Short works have appeared on-line in Camroc Press Review, Six Sentences, and Pine Tree Mysteries and most recently in the Gumshoe Review. Short stories have been published in various anthologies

Virginia blogs about writing and other interests, including genealogy, current events and gardening. She also posts book reviews, and some of her photography.

For more information or to contact Virginia,

virginiawinters.ca
vwinters@bell.net

Turn the page for an excerpt from Anne's next Dangerous Journey.

A DANGEROUS JOURNEYS MYSTERY

THE CHILD ON THE TERRACE

BOOK 4

VIRGINIA WINTERS

T he Andalusian donkey is patient and strong, a very kind animal that can become attached to one person.

Day One and Two

Anne waited for a taxi to take her from the airport to a hotel in the center of old Madrid. Around her, Spanish voices mixed with English and German and many others. Strangers all. She passed her hand over a bronze, erotic statue of a woman astride a bull. Sunshine bounced from its polished surface into her eyes, bringing unexpected tears. How she wished this were a simple vacation with Thomas, instead of a trip to mend her heart and forget him and the violence he brought into her life. She signaled the next car in the line of waiting taxis and gave the driver the address in central Madrid. After a shower and a change of clothes, she stepped from the doorway of her hotel into a maelstrom of people: tourists, police in their tiny vehicles, children and their parents, and one determined motorist who was backing out of a parking garage she'd entered in defiance of the no spaces sign.

Anne strolled down a cobblestoned city block and, beside a statue of Cortes, took in a view that included Neptune's fountain in the Plaza de Cibeles. Her goal for the afternoon was the Prado museum and the Velazquez painting Las Meninas said by many experts to be the most important painting in Europe, in part because of its influence on later artists such as Picasso. When she found it, she drifted in silence around the room devoted to the artist, stunned by the immediacy of the 400-year-old works.

Later, she sat on the boulevard at a cafe across from the museum, sipping a glass of juice and enjoying the street life. A young boy ran up to her, dropped a box on her table and scuttled off. She followed his progress across the broad avenue to the central promenade. A man waiting in the shade of a Sycamore tree, passed the boy something, money she supposed, and strode away to the entrance to the Prado. His face never turned towards her, but something about his walk was familiar. She opened the box to find a glass paperweight, the interior filled with purple and yellow violets, and a note.

Meet me at your hotel at 7 p.m.

Unsigned. The child must have mistaken her for someone else or the person who directed him had. No doubt she would be able to clear it up when whoever it was, arrived.

But no one showed at her hotel at 7 p.m., or later when she drank a glass of wine and watched the locals take back Plaza Sant' Ana from the tourists. Children played in the makeshift playground, even though it was almost 10 p.m. Normal for Spain, she thought.

Madrid was enduring a general strike. Helicopters buzzed overhead, flying in ominous formations of two or three, and from time to time police vehicles navigated through the crowded street. At one end of the plaza, on a makeshift stage, a band played protest songs from the sixties, in English; at the other three policemen stood, arrayed in polished boots and holstered sidearms, but not riot helmets or long guns, at ease, watching. After a time, bored, or so Anne thought, they moved on. Hawkers, emerging from the belly of the crowd, swarmed table after table, selling souvenirs and noise-makers. She returned to her hotel on the corner, with its minuscule elevator that she entered one way and exited another.

From her terrace, as large as the room itself, she listened to the music and the voices of the crowd. Later she woke from a nightmare of the room in Bermuda where she had fired at the man who tried to kill her. The plaza, quieter now, soothed her with distant voices and snatches of music, and she slept again.

The next morning, she waited in the Atocha station for the AVE train that would take her south to Seville. Alberto de Palacio Elissagne and Gustave Eiffel designed the building in a wrought-iron renewal style when it was rebuilt in 1892 after a fire. The glass and iron roof rose above a botanical garden. Anne wandered along, taken away from the bustle of the passengers thronging to the trains by the woody smell of the gardens. At one end a gentle fountain tumbled into a pool covered in green vegetation. Part of the green climbed onto the rocks and Anne realized turtles swam under the mantle of the plants.

Charmed, she sat on a bench beside the garden until time to take the train.

The AVE covered the almost six hundred kilometers from Madrid to Seville in less than three hours. Only the trees and vineyards whipping by indicated the speed. Anne slept, waking as the train arrived in Seville. She stayed in a hotel close to the bus station and left the next morning for the Andalusian city of Ronda and on to Setenil where she had rented a house for two months of repair work on her emotions.

The countryside changed, revealing olive trees in plantations that climbed up steep hills, turning them a soft blue-green. Smoke from the autumn pruning lingered in the valleys. The hills became mountains and the road more perilous but the driver, one hand on the wheel, took the turns at what seemed to Anne a breakneck speed. Another, slower country bus wound its way to Setenil.

The white villages of Andalusia, carved out of mountainsides, ravaged by war, carried on a relaxed pace of life she wanted to enter, to lose herself in and heal. Setenil, inhabited since Roman times and perhaps long before, overlooked the Rio Trajo. The facades of the older homes hid living spaces carved from the rock itself. Seven times the Christian kings tried to wrest it from the Moors, only succeeding late in the Reconquista, the long war that took Spain back from the invaders. It was easy to see why, Anne thought, as she walked the steep hill from the bus stop to the plaza and beyond to the villa she had rented.

The owner met her at the front of a whitewashed house set into the rock.

"Welcome, Doctor McPhail." The English voices in cafes, shops and now, here, startled her, even though she knew many British settled in Spain when the establishment of the EU passport made travel and emigration so easy.

Anne shook hands with her host, a woman who towered eight inches over her own five foot two.

"Would you like to come through?"

They stepped across a stone terrace to a blue, rough-hewn wooden door that opened into a living room wide enough for a green sofa and two cream-colored chairs grouped before the fireplace. A cavity in the side of the fireplace promised a bread oven. A window to the front and one to the right of the doorway let in light, but even at noon, the interior remained darker than Anne preferred. A pot of red geraniums set on the dining table lent a peppery scent to the house. All the necessary elements crammed a kitchen the size of a walk-in closet. A powder room was tucked under the staircase. One floor up, a room with a double bed opened to a minute balcony, its railing draped with more scarlet geraniums. A bathroom, complete with shower, finished the tour.

"I'm sorry there's no bath," her landlady said.

"Suits me very well," Anne said.

She wanted the woman to finish the business, to leave her in this cocoon of a house, to sort out her memories and her doubts.

Alone, she divided her clothes between a white chest of drawers and an armoire. A check of the kitchen revealed a need to shop.

The owner left behind a binder full of suggestions: where to eat, where to buy food and wine, and what attractions to see. Stepping from the dark interior into the street, she waited for her eyes to adjust to the intense light reflected from the exteriors of the houses that had received their summer coat of white paint, joining them to a tradition of the villages in Andalusia which shone like beacons along the dark mountainsides.

A few steps brought her to a plaza, large enough for a terrace restaurant. A stone wall prevented a dozen tables, sheltered under an immense overhang of rock, from tumbling into the river far below. More tables clustered near the entrance to the cafe, across a narrow roadway, infrequently bothered by cars and most often, as now, used as a playground for children. When a car did appear, calls from mothers and older children scattered the younger ones to the side, like a group of boys playing hockey on a suburban Canadian street, calling "car, car" and racing to move the nets.

She ordered a glass of white wine, sat back in her chair and took her first free breath since she left Bermuda.

One of the dozen or so children, a girl perhaps five years old, with red hair tied back in a ponytail, stood watching the others. The young woman with her, not her mother, Anne thought, tossed her long dark hair and chattered with the man who sat at their table. She shooed the child away towards the other children.

The little girl sidled around the edge of a group of three others of about the same age. They stopped playing with their dolls, fell silent and watched her. She drifted away, towards Anne's table.

"Hello," said Anne. Before she could switch to Spanish, the little girl answered.

"Hello," she said in British-accented English. "What's your name?"

"My name is Anne."

"My name is...Maria Sophia."

Her minder looked around, leaped up and ran over to her, chiding her in angry Spanish for talking to strangers. At least Anne caught the word "estranja" and knew that meant stranger.

"I'm sorry—" Anne began, but the girl hissed, tossed her hair, grabbed Maria's hand and hauled her away.

The waiter bustled up to her table, apologizing. "I am sorry, Senora. Maria Sophia is not allowed to speak to the tourists."

"That's okay. I shouldn't have answered her but the other children wouldn't play with her."

The waiter leaned closer and lowered his voice. "They don't

think she's Spanish. They think she's Basque and have been told not to play with her."

"What have they got against the Basque?"

"Some of us lost family in the terrorist attacks."

"Esti is not her mother?"

"No, no." Another couple sat down, and he drifted away.

Esti was Basque, but the child... None of her business. Her business was to sort out her emotions and her beliefs after the episode in Bermuda. She hadn't talked to Thomas since.